DEDICATION

For my daughter & granddaughter –
May you never let anyone shadow your light or silence your voice.
Ever.

How to Stay Out of Prison: A Modern-Day Woman's Guide

M.E. Clayton

Copyright © 2019 Monica Clayton

All rights reserved.

ISBN: 978-1-64570-426-3

CONTENTS

	Acknowledgments	i
	Prologue	Pg #1
1	Lyrical	Pg #3
2	Nixon	Pg #7
3	Lyrical	Pg #11
4	Nixon	Pg #15
5	Lyrical	Pg #19
6	Nixon	Pg #23
7	Lyrical	Pg #27
8	Nixon	Pg #31
9	Lyrical	Pg #35
10	Nixon	Pg #39
11	Lyrical	Pg #43
12	Nixon	Pg #47
13	Lyrical	Pg #51
14	Nixon	Pg #55
15	Lyrical	Pg #59
16	Nixon	Pg #63
17	Lyrical	Pg #67
18	Nixon	Pg #71
19	Lyrical	Pg #75
20	Nixon	Pg #79

21	Lyrical	Pg #83
22	Nixon	Pg #87
23	Lyrical	Pg #91
24	Nixon	Pg #95
25	Lyrical	Pg #99
	Epilogue	Pg #103
	About the Author	Pg #106
	Other Books	Pg #107

ACKNOWLEDGMENTS

The first acknowledgment will always be my husband. There aren't enough words to express my gratitude for having this man in my life. There is a little bit of him in every hero that I dream up, and I can't thank God enough for bringing him into my life.

Second, there's my family; my daughter, my son, my grandchildren, my sister, and my mother. Family is everything, and I have one of the best. They are truly the best cheerleaders I could ever ask for, and I never forget just how truly blessed I am to have them in my life.

Then, of course, there's Kamala. This woman is not only my beta and idea guinea pig, but she's also one of my closest friends. She's been with me from the beginning of this journey, and we're going to ride this thing to the end. Kam's the encouragement that sparked it all, folks.

Finally, I'd like to thank everyone who's purchased, read, reviewed, shared, and supported me and my writing. Thank you so much for helping make this dream a reality and a happy, fun one at that. I cannot say thank you enough.

PROLOGUE

Lyrical – (9-years-old) ~
This was dumb.
    They were dumb.
    I mean, nothing they were saying was making any sense to me.
    "But…Aunt Blanche asked us how she looked in her big purple dress," I argued. "I just answered her question."
    My mom closed her blue eyes as she let out one of those breaths that fill up your lungs too much. "Lyrical…"
    I crossed my arms over my chest, and I almost rolled my eyes, but my dad would spank me for that, so I didn't. "I don't understand, Mom," I said again. "You guys are acting like it's my fault she looks like a big, wrinkly, purple plum in that dress."
    Dad laughed, and Mom shot him that look that she always did when he was in trouble but didn't want to get him in trouble in front of us. Dad immediately stopped laughing, then Mom turned back to me. "Lyric, honey," she said, using her soft voice. "I know it might be hard for you to understa-"
    I started shaking my head at her. "You're not supposed to lie," I reminded her. "You and Dad tell me all the time that I'm not supposed to lie." I looked between my mom and dad to make sure that they knew that I did my best to listen to them when they told me stuff. "You guys told me that lying is wrong, and I'm supposed to always tell the truth."
    Mom closed her eyes again while Dad leaned forward with his elbows on his knees, his hands squeezing together. They were sitting on the couch, and I was sitting on the table that was always in the middle of our living room. They always sat me here when they needed to talk to me together.
    It sucked.
    I hated this table.
    "Lyric," Dad said, taking over where Mom left off, "I-*we* don't want you lying, that is true-"

"So, then—"

Dad put his hand up to stop me from talking. That was his nice way of telling us to shut up. "Lyrical, while it's true that lying is wrong, there are these things called little white lies, and people tell them when they don't want to hurt someone's feelings."

I didn't understand.

I tilted my head to the side. "But isn't lying still hurting someone's feelings?" I asked. "I mean, if you lied to Mom about something, wouldn't her feelings be hurt if she found out you lied?"

I watched as my parents shared a look, and I squinted my eyes at them. They were trying to trick me; I just knew it.

Mom did that breathing thing again. "It's not that simple, Lyric," she said, trying to explain her point. "While lying is wrong, sometimes you can tell a little fib, so that no one's feelings get hurt."

I uncrossed my arms, then threw them up in the air. "I don't understand," I said again. "Isn't it better for me to tell Aunt Blanche that she looks like a big, wrinkly, purple plum, so that she can change, instead of letting her walk around looking like a big, wrinkly, purple plum?" I shrugged a shoulder. "I mean, that seems more mean to me than telling her the truth." I looked at my dad and ignored my mom's prayers.

"Jesus Christ," he mumbled.

My eyes widened. "You're not supposed to use The Lord's name in vain," I reminded him.

I watched as my father ran both his hands through his thick brown hair, and then down his face. "Lyric, you're killing me here, sweetie," he said, shaking his head.

I crossed my arms over my chest again. "What do you guys want me to do?" I knew that I wasn't supposed to lie, but I didn't want to get in trouble by my parents, either. "Do I tell the truth or don't I?"

"It's not that simple, Lyric," my mother tried to explain again.

"It should be," I grumbled.

"Yes, it should," my father agreed. "It should be, but life isn't always black and white."

I was so confused.

"What does that mean?"

My mother sighed. "It just means that you need to think about your words before you say them."

This felt like a trick.

"So, do I get in trouble for lying or don't I?" I asked because I needed to know.

"It depends on the lie, Lyric," my father said.

"That's not fair!"

"Life never is, honey," my father said.

CHAPTER 1

Lyrical – (Twenty Years Later) ~
I laid in bed, looking up at the ceiling, trying to recall where on the list of Commandments did murder rank.
Was it the first Commandment?
I mean, if it was first on the list, then I could see that'd be a super no-no, but if it wasn't first...
However, my thoughts were interrupted again by *another* opening of the door where laughter, music, and partying snuck through, rattling my walls.
Screw this.
I reached over towards my nightstand, then grabbed my phone. The traitorous screen screamed that it was 1:14 am, but I pretended not to see it as I tapped on the search bar. Then, as if I had all the time in the world, my fingers flew across the screen, typing in The Ten Commandments, and Thall Shall Not Kill was number six on the list.
It was number *six*.
It didn't even rank in the top five.
So, surely, it wasn't that bad of an offense, right? I mean, if I was lucky enough to make it to The Pearly Gates, then I could easily explain how it'd been totally reasonable to kill my neighbor. He was rude as hell with no thoughts of anyone but himself, and if I stayed true to the other nine Commandments, then that should even out the scales, shouldn't it?
I'd been living in my building for over five years already, and I'd never had one complaint to mutter about. The building was a high-rise of spaciously rent-controlled apartments that I'd been lucky enough to land a space in. The building's structure had always been sturdy, clean, and well maintained, and the rooms were bigger than a shoebox, which was a treasure all its own. So, I knew how lucky I was to live in this building.
I did.
Especially, when I didn't make a whole lot as a pet store manager. Still, it

was just me, so I got along fine. At least, I *had been* getting along fine until Bruce Higgins moved in across the hallway about a month ago, and it wasn't that he'd just moved in.

No.

He moved in because he was fortunate enough to be banging the building manager, Randall Smyth. I'd found that little tidbit out the first night that Bruce had thrown a party (on a Tuesday), and I had *calmly* knocked on his door to ask him to keep it down. Some fuckface partier had opened the door, and when I had *politely* asked him if they could keep it down, he had laughed in my face, then had told me to take it up with the apartment manager right before he had slammed the door in my face.

Now, stop!

Here's the part where you'd probably want to push him aside, step into the apartment, then scream out a lecture at the top of your lungs on basic consideration, but you don't.

You don't because you don't know the people in attendance, and it takes only one person to come at you all crazy, inciting you to pop them one in the face. In turn, that leads to a night-*or two*-sitting in a jail cell, possible bail, and an assault and battery charge. So, as that one day in March (when I'd been fourteen) had taught me, that wasn't how I'd wanted to spend my Tuesday night.

So, instead, I had marched over to Mr. Smyth's office first thing the next morning to log an official complaint. Like an asshole, he'd been quick to accuse me of being homophobic and resenting a party attended by mostly gay people. I'd been offended at his offendedness but had kept my mouth shut because I hadn't wanted to get kicked out of my apartment. It hadn't been until a couple of days later, when I'd seen Bruce and Randall kissing through the opened crack of Bruce's door, that I'd realized that I was screwed.

Since then, I'd been trying to live life on lack of sleep so severe that it was a miracle that I could even still dress myself at this point. There were permanent bags under my brown eyes and there wasn't enough concealer in the world to erase them. However, the great thing about my job was that I spent most of it in my office, and so I didn't have to interact with people a whole lot. Whenever I did emerge from behind my desk, I spent a lot of time checking on the animals that we sold at the pet store.

Through happy happenstance, I managed A Pet's Love, a pet store that was divided into four sections. Like most pet stores, the store front housed pet supplies as far as the eye could see. However, the back was sectioned off into two areas: one housed the animals that we sold, and the other housed my office, the employees' restroom, and the employees' break room, even though a lot of employees spent their breaks playing with the animals. Now, unlike most pet stores, the south end of the building housed our veterinarian clinic, and we had an on-site veterinarian, and he had one assistant. A Pet's Love really was a one-stop shop for any pet lover.

I'd started working there shortly after I had dropped out of college. I had managed to credit myself with two years of a college education, but once I realized how tight my parents had been stretching themselves after sending my sister, Alice, to college, I had dropped out.

My parents had felt horrible, but not as horrible as I'd felt finding out how in debt they had been. Nevertheless, it hadn't been an impulsive decision. Before I had officially dropped out, I'd done the math and had even taken on a couple of jobs to try to make it happen, but college was an expensive mofo.

So, after that, I had worked odd jobs until about five years ago, when I'd gotten hired at A Pet's Love. I had worked hard, then had made manager after two years, and the promotion had given me enough of a raise to actually be able to live a decent life.

I thought often about going back to college, but if the price had been sky-high ten years ago, then I couldn't even begin to imagine what it cost now. Plus, I was happy. I guess that's why it was more of a fanciful idea than an actual urge. If I was unhappy in life, then maybe I'd be more apt to take going back to college more seriously, but I wasn't unhappy, and I had a good life. I had great parents that loved me, an awesome sister that was changing the world, and I also had a best friend that I knew for a fact would sit in a jail cell with me if the night deemed it so.

Now, while I didn't have a boyfriend, that was okay. I mean, I didn't have anything against them, but I liked my life stress-free, not that men automatically equaled stress, mind you. I just didn't feel like taking the chance.

The door opened again, and I wondered if I was going to become an episode on Fear Thy Neighbor.

I placed my phone back on the nightstand, then pushed my earplugs farther into my ear canal. Would I go deaf some day? Probably. Nevertheless, sleep was the goal right now. So, I rolled over to my side, then nested my head onto the pillow, grabbing the extra pillow that occupied the empty side of my queen-size bed, so that I could throw it over my head.

The party was in full swing, and the only thing keeping me from going over there-*besides jail*-was the fact that I was being sent on a managers' conference in St. Louis, Missouri tomorrow. The travel was far enough from Chicago to warrant an overnight stay with free accommodations, and that was a blessing because that meant sleep.

Blessed, peaceful, beautiful sleep.

I'd be flying back on Friday afternoon, which meant that tonight and Thursday night were going to be full of sleep and more sleep. Hell, I might do nothing but sleep while I was away. Screw seeing the sights. Who needed to see the sights? Not this girl. This girl needed some goddamn sleep.

As I laid in my bed-not sleeping-I contemplated sleeping pills. However, I wasn't a fan and hated the idea of drugging my body. I also didn't want to become addicted to them or read in ten years that my intestines were going to melt inside my body when they discovered that the sleeping pills were actually a toxic poison that I had voluntarily taken.

Super dramatic? Probably.

Still, that's what lack of sleep did to a person. That's why they used it as a prisoner tactic when they captured the enemy. Sleep deprivation was a real method of torture. Like legit. So, right now, Bruce was actually torturing me. Like really torturing me as defined by our American government.

So, if I was being tortured, didn't I have the right to defend myself? Didn't I have the right to save myself from unspeakable torture by an asshole that had no concept of basic neighborly consideration? If you asked me, then the answer was yes.

Plus, it'd already been established that Thall Shall Not Kill was number six on the list. So, if I killed Bruce in self-defense to end his legally sanctioned torture…well, then, Thall Shall Not Kill should rank even further down the list, right?"

However, did multiple kills move it back up the list?

Because, as I gave it some more thought, wouldn't I also have to kill Randall since he was an accomplice? I mean, I couldn't let him move someone else in that also liked to party until the break of dawn, right? After all, someone had to put an end to Randall's abuse of power. Someone had to fight for the cause, and it looked like that someone was going to have to be me.

I sighed.

I should probably reevaluate my reasoned killing spree after I had a couple decent nights of sleep, see how I still felt afterwards. So, the plan was to fly to St. Louis this afternoon, sleep, give my all to the meetings, sleep, give some more of my all, sleep, then fly home and hopefully not kill anyone.

CHAPTER 2

Nixon ~

"We have a problem," Abbi Lewis said in lieu of her usual professional morning greeting.

I walked past her, then straight into my office, but I knew that she would follow like she did every morning. Normally, it was with a morning greeting and a rundown of what the day looked like, but I guess today was looking to be anything but normal.

"Oh, really?"

"Yep," she replied.

I placed my briefcase on my desk, then turned to face her. "So, what is it?"

Abbi walked up to me with her hand stretched out, handing me some papers. "The building manager for the apartments on Canal Street moved his boyfriend into apartment 4D, and he's waiving his rent, letting him throw parties every night, and basically letting him get away with murder."

I grabbed the papers, then scanned over them lightly, though I didn't really need to read her reports. Abbi wasn't one for extra flair, so whatever she said was usually on her reports, word-for-word. "How do you know Randall's letting all of that take place? Maybe he's clueless about his newest tenant."

Abbi cocked her head, looking at me like I was an idiot. "Good old-fashion gossip, Nixon," she answered. "I have a friend who lives in that building, and she and Bruce-that's the boytoy, by the way-have become friends of sorts. Apparently, Bruce isn't big on discretion, and he's been bragging to anyone that will listen about how he has it made as long as he keeps sucking Randall's dick."

Fuck.

I'd gotten into real estate seven years ago on a fluke, and for the most part, it'd been a positive and profitable direction for me. I had graduated college with degrees in finance and architectural engineering with some grandiose idea of living my life by creating magnificent buildings. However, that shit had come to a quick halt when it'd become obvious that I didn't work well with others. My vision was my vision, and my vision alone, so I had struggled with suggestions and direction from others. Word of advice: architecture was not the choice career for someone that couldn't work well with others.

So, seven years ago, I'd been stuck in traffic when a rundown corner building had caught my eye. I'd sat in my car, staring at it for a while-*mostly because traffic had been at a standstill*-then had started to envision everything that could be done to it. That night, I had called around to find out who owned the building, and with the help of my brothers, I had purchased my first flip property.

The experience had been an entirely different kind of involvement from creating something from scratch. I'd been limited to what I could do with the building's structure, and believe it or not, that had helped me get over my aversion to taking suggestions and the like. Granted, I still had final say over what any of my buildings would eventually represent, but I wasn't a dick about it anymore.

Well, not much of a dick.

Now, seven years later, I had paid my brothers back, flipped more buildings than I could count, and own multiple commercial and residential buildings, apartment buildings included.

I shook my head. "Why would Randall risk his job for a hookup?" I mean, I was all for scratching that sexual itch, but to risk losing your job and home for it? No pussy was that good.

Abbi cocked her head to the other side. "You've obviously never had a good dicking," she said sardonically. Abbi wasn't one to mince words.

I cocked a brow. "And I never will," I replied, making sure that we were clear on my sexual preferences. While I had nothing against how people got down, I was attracted to women *only*.

"So, what do you want to do about this?" she asked, getting back to business.

I employed enough people that I could have any one of my senior property managers handle it, but I didn't like putting them in sticky situations. When dealing with evictions, property damage, etc., I liked to be involved, so that I knew what to expect should I have to make an appearance in court later, and this was no different.

If what Abbi was reporting was true-*and I was pretty sure that it was because Abbi didn't exaggerate*-I'd be evicting two people from my building today. The Canal property fell under Sebastian Steele's (his name really was suited for adult films) portfolio. "Let me call Bast, then we'll head on over and pay Randall a visit," I answered.

Abbi nodded. "Okay. You're clear after the senior staff meeting, but only for an hour," she informed me. "You have to meet with Grace Properties at eleven o'clock."

I glanced at my watch, then back over at Abbi. "Is there anything pressing on the staff meeting agenda this morning?"

Mondays were usually our most detailed staff meetings since we didn't work the weekends. So, the rest of the week was basically just touching base with whatever shit was going on. Since today was Wednesday, I couldn't imagine anything dire being discussed today.

"No," Abbi said, confirming my thoughts. "Just the usual."

"Good," I replied. "Send out a senior staff email, cancelling today's meeting, please."

"Sure thing, boss. Go get 'em," she teased.

I smiled as I watched her walk out of my office. Abbi was an honest-to-goodness godsend. She had to be the most organized person on the planet, and she was just as ferocious in her quest to maintain order. No one-save for family-saw me without an appointment, and she did her best to run my life smoothly. Her only concession was that the weekends were hers. She was willing to work sixteen-hour days during the week, but her weekends were untouchable.

So, while everyone else might get a random call on their days off, Abbi didn't. She'd made it very clear that nothing and no one was more important to her than her family, so Saturdays and Sundays belonged to her husband and children. Coming from a close family myself, I respected her stipulation. Plus, five years later, she had more than proven her worth.

I dropped down on my chair, then reached for my desk phone. It was only eight in the morning, but most of my staff was already up and running by now, so I wasn't surprised when Sebastian answered on the third ring.

"What's up, boss?"

I skipped the greeting. "I just got a report that Randall Smyth accepted a new tenant in the Canal building, and in exchange for some…uh, romance, he's letting the tenant live there rent-free, and he's reportedly throwing parties every night and whatnot."

"Goddamn it," Bast grumbled. "Are you sure? I mean, I know your reports are usually spot on, but Randall's always been good to S.J.S."

"Well, according to Abbi, love is blind," I retorted.

Bast snorted. "Not as blind as lust, that's for sure."

I ignored his comparison. "Want to take a drive with me?"

"I wouldn't miss this for free tickets to a Victoria Secret's fashion show," he joked, and I couldn't help shaking my head.

Unfortunately, most of my senior staff had seen me lose my shit in technicolor once or twice before, so Sebastian's glee was real. Apparently, my loss of composure was entertaining, and Abbi had mentioned once before that I should sell tickets.

The assholes.

"Meet me in the garage in ten," I said right before hanging up on him. Abbi was probably my closest friend in the building, so to everyone else, I was the boss, which usually led me to skipping the niceties.

I grabbed my cellphone next, then dialed my brother, Lincoln. When he answered, I cut right to the chase because Lincoln didn't have a lot of free time. "I'm on my way to evict a couple of tenants, so I might need your assistance later."

His laughter chimed through the phone. "Can I go?"

Goddamn it.

"No," I growled. "You cannot go."

"Awwwwe, c'mon, Nix," he whined. "I've been on vacation since Monday, and I've had no drama to keep me occupied since." Linc was a criminal defense attorney, and one of the best in the state. I wasn't just saying that as his brother, either; I was saying it because it was true. Also, his hourly rate was proof of it.

"I can't believe you make your living upholding the law," I remarked. "Shouldn't you be talking me out of going there?" No one knew my temper like my brothers.

Lincoln was thirty-five with his own partnered law firm, and it was weird to associate him with such a serious profession sometimes. Linc was all charm and smoothness, and he had the best sense of humor, trying not to take life too seriously. Nevertheless, once you got him in the courtroom, he turned into one of the most vicious creatures around.

As for my other brother, Jackson, he was the oldest at thirty-seven, and he was Dad's junior. He was a pediatric doctor and *very* serious, but I supposed that you had to be in his line of work. Plus, being the oldest brother, he'd always been more mature than me and Linc. Jackson also loved kids, so he took their health and wellbeing very much to heart. Now, while abuse cases tended to send him over the edge, for the most part, Jackson was well-balanced and happy, if not a little…rigid.

I was also happy. It was just when I wasn't that I turned into a world-class dick. However, I was working on that. It was probably why, at thirty-three, I'd yet to settle down. Not too many women wanted to tie themselves to a jerk.

"Why would I talk you out of it?" Linc asked, bringing me back to the topic at hand. "That's more money for me if you do lose your shit, little brother."

"You're a dick," I snorted.

"Takes one to know one," he sing-songed.

I sighed. "Just be…available."

"Of course," he replied like I knew he would.

The only problem with having a brother that was a criminal defense attorney? It gave you the false illusion that you could punch your way out of anything.

CHAPTER 3

Lyrical ~
It was Friday afternoon, and I was eyeing my apartment building like it was Satan come to life.

I had just spent the last two nights living in a miracle of clean sheets, fluffy pillows, a sturdy but willowy mattress, and honest-to-goodness sleep.

Restful sleep.

I'd finally gotten some actual sleep, not the kind that was plagued with tossing and turning. I hadn't even minded the long meeting days because I'd been able to go back to my hotel room and sleep. Though my colleagues had tried to get me to go out and see the sights, I had held strong. Sleep was more important to me at this stage in my life than seeing the sights of a place that I didn't care about. Now, while I was absolutely positive that St. Louis was a beautiful city, it just wasn't more beautiful than sleep; nothing was.

However, now I was back home in Satan's alley.

Okay, that wasn't fair.

It was more like Satan's floor because the misery didn't take up an entire alley.

Granted, thanks to the restful sleep that I had managed to get, I'd been able to place Bruce's murder on the back burner, finally realizing that killing him would probably gift me with more problems than just a few sleepless nights. Still, the idea was just placed on the back burner for now, not ruled out entirely.

I dragged my rollaway behind me, then trudged up the stairs into the building. Walking through the lobby, I hated how, once upon a time, I'd been able to appreciate everything about the building and my luck at living here. However, now I dreaded the journey to my apartment.

Along with the sleep that I had managed to rack up these past two nights, I had also seriously contemplated if I should take my complaints directly to the building's owner. I mean, Randall had to answer to someone, right? There had to be someone that made sure Randall was doing his job, I would think.

Sighing out my despair, I knew that I couldn't afford to pass up the mailboxes since I'd been gone for two days. We had standard apartment mailboxes that lined the north end of the lobby, and while they were decent sized, I wasn't sure how long they could hold all my junk mail. After all, I very rarely got any real mail.

After gathering all my mail-*and, yes, it was all junk mail*-I walked over towards the elevator for my ascent back up to the floor that housed Hell. I waited patiently for the steel box of doom, contemplating the best way to go about reporting Bruce and Randall, when I noticed the sexiest man on the planet approaching, presumably to wait for the elevator as well.

Now, stop!

With his dark, styled, chestnut-brown hair, bright hazel eyes, and tall, muscular, fit build, you might want to just grab the man, then climb him like a spider monkey, but don't.

Believe it or not, just touching someone could be considered assault. That's right. You could reach out and just poke someone's arm, but if they took offense to it, they could actually file a police report accusing you of assault.

I mean, what bullshit, right?

Because if anyone should be being touched, it was the six-foot-something of male perfection that was standing next to me and was also waiting for the elevator. However, instead of jumping his person, I decided to just peek subtle glances up at him, hoping that he didn't catch me ogling his hot body.

When the elevator doors opened, I went to take a step forward, and Sexy-Man extended his arm out, saying, "After you."

I looked up at him, ready to smile and say thank you, but my voice got caught somewhere in the pit of my stomach. The man was smiling down at me, and he was way better looking than I had originally given him credit for. Seriously, the man was freakin' beautiful.

After a bunch of mindless gurgles-*because who could speak at a time like this*-this god of a man grabbed my suitcase, then placing his hand on the small of my back, he ushered me into the elevator. No one else entered behind us, and once the doors slid shut, he faced the numbered panel, then asked, "What floor?"

"Four," I mumbled, completely embarrassed. I could only imagine what I looked like after traveling, and it was just my luck that I'd meet up with a goddamn Greek god.

I watched as he pressed the button for the fourth floor only, meaning that he was going to my floor, too. Was he a new tenant?

God, please, let him be a new tenant.

Honestly, living in the same building as this man might make up for Bruce and Randall's evil ways.

Sexy-Man still had a hold of my rollaway when he asked, "Would you like some help with this once we get to our floor?"

I looked up at him, and I swear to God, his eyes must emit magic because I couldn't summon up one single thought in my head other than how gorgeous this man was. Now, of course, I didn't need help with my rollaway, but I still wasn't sure how to answer. Did I say yes and adopt the helpless female persona, or say no and adopt the independent female persona?

I mean, my simple reply could be life-altering if I could determine which kind of female he was drawn to, right? We could end up telling our grandchildren how we met at an elevator, or forty years from now, I could end up telling my seven cats how he was the one who got away.

After a few awkward seconds, I decided on independent female. "Uh…" I had to clear my throat. "Thank you, but I can manage."

Sexy-Man smiled. "Okay," he said. "But it's no trouble if you'd like some help."

When the elevator dinged, he stepped back, then let me exit first, but before I could introduce myself and thank him for his offer, his phone rang. He looked at me apologetically as he dug his phone out of his pocket, then looking at the screen, he grimaced. "Sorry, I have to take this," he whispered to me.

Now, stop!

Right now, you might want to reach out to slap his phone out of his hand and demand that he fall in love with you, but you can't do that. If his phone broke when it hit the floor, then that was destruction of property, and while that might not come with a court date, it did come with a fine. So, instead of demanding all his attention, I smiled, waved, then headed down the hallway to my apartment, hoping that he lived in the building, so that we could fall in love later when he wasn't so preoccupied.

I reached the door to my apartment, unlocked it, then rolled my luggage inside. I shut the door behind me, headed straight for the bedroom, then began unpacking my rollaway and putting all my toiletries up. I threw all my dirty clothes in the hamper, then realized that I was going to have to do laundry soon. I didn't have a washer and dryer, but the building did have a mini-laundromat in the basement. The basement also had extra storage units that you could pay to rent. Still, that was as far as the amenities went; there was no gym, spa, or pool in the building. Though it was a nice apartment complex, it wasn't anything near luxury-condo like.

Once all my crap was put away, I grabbed a towel from the linen closet, then headed towards the bathroom. I had no idea what it was about your home shower, but no matter how luxurious your hotel shower might be, nothing felt better than coming home from a long trip and taking a hot shower in your own familiar watery surroundings.

I took a shower long enough to offend water conservationists everywhere, but I didn't care. Sometimes you had to sacrifice for the sake of sanity, and I took my sanity very seriously.

Wrapping myself up in towels of fluffiness, I went back into the bedroom, then picked up my phone to look at the time. It was only four in the afternoon with the sun still out, but I was so exhausted that I threw on a tank-top, a pair of panties, some pajama pants, and after towel drying my hair, I threw it up in a damp bun.

I didn't bother with a bra because my girls didn't need to be contained that way. I had a respectable B-cup, but they hadn't been attacked by gravity or childbirth yet, so they still held impressively without a bra.

It was my ass, hips, and thighs that needed to be controlled more than anything else. I had your classic pear-shaped physique, and being only five-foot-four-inches, my lower half looked thicker than I'd like, but there wasn't much That I could do about it.

Walking towards the kitchen, I had grand plans to make a nice cup of tea, find a corny, awful, low-budget horror movie, then just empty my mind for the rest of the day. However, all those plans came to an abrupt halt when I heard... *hammering?*...coming from across the hallway.

Now, while I understood that it was only four in the afternoon, and while I understood that the sun was still out, and that people were living their lives in ways that daylight hours allowed them, that hammering was ruining my plans for a relaxing afternoon.

Again, I understood that it was only four, but something about that hammering noise making its way over here to ruin my plans of rest and relaxation snapped something inside my head. I mean, I actually felt something snap. Plus, the twitch in my eye was a sure sign of some sort of mental collapse, right? The grinding of my teeth and balled-up fists were also other indicators that I wasn't in my right mind. Surely, a mental break could be the only reason why I did what I did next.

There was no other explanation.

After working so hard all these years to stay out of prison, too.

Go figure.

CHAPTER 4

Nixon ~
When Linc had told me that I was stupid for cleaning up this shit myself, I should have given his criticism some credit, because it'd been three days already and this shit was going to run into tomorrow afternoon for sure.

Randall Smyth had still been in his pajamas when Sabastian and I had knocked on his door Wednesday morning. He'd looked surprised to see me, but that surprise had quickly given way to nervousness when I'd told him that I knew about his rent-free tenant. I'd learned over the years that the best approach when dealing with shady people was to be confident with your accusations; never give the other person a chance to make up some bullshit that might put a dent in your mission.

After telling Randall that I knew about Bruce, I had ordered him to walk with me to Bruce's apartment, then-after *a lot* of theatrics from Bruce-both men had agreed to leave peacefully, rather than to have to face charges of theft, fraud, vandalism, and trespassing.

The downside was that after Bruce had vacated the apartment, and I'd finally gotten a chance to do a walk-through, I had quickly discovered that the rumors of his partying hadn't been exaggerated. The apartment had been a fucking mess and needed some work. There'd even been a couple of cabinet doors hanging from their hinges.

I'd been so fucking pissed that I had opted to work off my irritation by doing the work myself. I had worked a half-day Wednesday, Thursday, and today, and then I had called Linc to help me since he was on vacation. Jackson had even stopped by for a few hours yesterday to help out as well.

I had just finished hammering in a new baseboard when Lincoln started bitching again. "I still can't believe I let you talk me into helping you with this bullshit," he griped. "I'm supposed to be on vacation."

"Quit bitching," I replied. "Besides, it'll keep you humble."

Lincoln scoffed. "I'm humble plenty. If it wasn't for that sexy brunette that I ran into in the lobby, this entire day would have sucked."

I was about to comment when the front door was slapped open so hard that it bounced against the door frame, then swung back. I turned to see a very petite and pissed off ball of fury storming my way.

What the fuck?

She stopped in front of me, planted her hands on her hips, then did her best to burn her hate into me. "Look, I get that you might be feeling like a prince with free reign of the castle because you've got great cock sucking skills that Randall benefits from, but there is such a thing as common goddamn courtesy, you know."

My brows shot straight upward as my hands came up in a calming motion. "Whoa, hold on there-"

"I will not hold on," she snapped. "Just because you're screwing Randall, making you safe from eviction, does not mea-"

I stared at the beautiful woman, completely dumbfounded, as she finally took in Linc-*with his shirt off*-and her eyes rounded to impossible proportions. Seriously. I thought her eyes were going to pop right out of her pretty little head.

"Oh, my God!" she shrieked. "Randall is giving you a free apartment and unlimited sex, and you can't even bother to be faithful to him?!" She removed one hand off her hip, then gestured towards Linc. "Do you just sleep with any man who you can fleece?"

Who the hell was this woman?

"First off, I'm not gay," I said, finally snapping out of my shock. "I don-"

"You're not gay?!" she screeched as her pretty brown eyes *really* threatened to pop out of her head now. "Holy shit…are you just such an opportunist that you'd sleep with men when you're not even gay just to benefit from them?"

I stepped towards her until I was towering over her. "I do not sleep with men for-"

"Awe, sweet pea, don't be like that," Lincoln cooed from where he was standing.

I turned to look at him, my face incredulous that he would dare joke at a time like this. I was getting cussed out by a woman that I didn't know, and he was playing into her accusations for his own personal entertainment. "Do you fucking mind?"

Linc shrugged a shoulder but smiled all the same. "Not at all."

"Look," she continued, "I don't care who you sleep with or why. What I care about is all your goddamn partying and the lack of sleep it's causing me. I mean, Christ, how can you be so goddamn inconsiderate of your neighbors?"

Okay.

She obviously thought that I was Bruce, and it was apparent that she'd reached her limit on how much more she was going to take from him. It made sense, and I actually felt bad that I had let Randall's mismanagement go unnoticed for so long. So, I may have deserved to get cussed out, but she was cussing me out for the wrong reasons.

"Look, I-"

This time, she actually poked me in the chest. "No. *You* look," she seethed. "Since the day you moved in, I've had a total of about ten hours of sleep, and it stops now."

Her words were registering-*I swear, they were*-but the second that she jabbed me in the chest with her finger, her touch brought on an entirely new set of issues that I didn't know how to deal with right now. I wasn't sure if it was the contact of her finger, the shock wearing off, or the realization that she thought that I was Bruce, but all of a sudden, I noticed that the little ball of hate and accusations was clad in only a tank-top and pajama pants. With my mind finally alert and my eyes focusing, I took in everything else about her.

She was no taller than five-foot-four was my guess. She had a tangle of wet brown strands perched on the top of her head, and her face was devoid of any makeup products whatsoever, and what a fucking face it was. She had identical brown arched brows that were sitting over a pair of stunning chocolate pools, and her lashes were unadorned, but full enough not to need any enhancement. She had a straight, slim nose centered between two rosy cheeks, and the only thing that I couldn't figure was if they were rosy because that was her natural complexion, or if they were rosy because she was pissed as hell.

That brought me to the lips that were spewing cuss words and resentment at me. They were both full with the lower lip slightly more plumped. Honestly, they looked fucking delicious. In fact, they looked like they belonged wrapped around my cock.

As my eyes traveled downward, it was then that my dick joined in the perusal my mind and eyes were taking. Her tits were bra-less with her nipples standing at attention, and my dick was noticing how they would fit perfectly in my hands. They weren't huge, but they also weren't small. They were actually fucking perfect for all the things that were now running through my mind.

Farther down, I saw how her waist tapered in, but then flared out into a set of holy-fuck-me hips. I wasn't able to check out her ass without looking like a certified creeper, but the pajamas that she was wearing did nothing to disguise the thickness of her hips and thighs, then suddenly, all I could think about was how comfortable those thighs would cradle me as I buried my face between her legs, which were just as perfect as the rest of her, right down to her bare feet with the yellow toenail polish and toe ring that she was sporting.

Of course, she thought that I was gay.

Or straight.

She thought that I was gay/straight and fucking the apartment manager for perks. She also thought that I was gay/straight, fucking the apartment manager while also having an affair on him...with my brother.

Jesus fucking Christ.

She was still poking my chest as she continued her rant. "Now, here's what's going to happen," she said menacingly. "You are going to limit your parties to the weekend and let the rest of us hardworking folks get some sleep during the week. If not, I'm going to go tell Randall that you're cheating on him."

I decided to clear this up, once and for all. "I'm not Bruce," I finally informed her.

Her chocolate spheres narrowed, and then she shot those babies towards my brother. "Oh, my god!" she cried, shrieking again as she directed her wrath his way. "What kind of monster are you? You were actually going to just stand there and let your lover take the blame, Bruce?"

Lincoln threw his hands up in a surrendering motion. "Oh, hey-"

"I can't believe you," she said, cutting him off, and the look that she gave him would have withered a lesser man. "And to think I actually thought you were hot and sexy in the elevator."

Lincoln went from defensive to intrigued in less than a second. "You think I'm sexy?"

My little resident psycho threw her hands up in utter disgust. "Unbelievable," she growled. "But, of course, what would you expect from a person with no common courtesy whatsoever." Her eyes darted back and forth between me and Linc before she finally said, "To hell with the both of you."

She turned around, then stormed out of the apartment, and when she did, I was finally able to get a look at that ass that I'd been so curious about.

Mother. Fucker.

After slamming the door behind her, Linc broke the silence. "Holy shit. That's the sexy brunette I was-"

"Back off. She's mine," I growled as I looked back over at my brother.

Linc smirked. "I'm pretty sure she said she thought I was sexy, so-"

"Don't make me have to explain to Mom why she's down one son," I threatened.

My brother let out a low whistle. "Damn," he rushed out. "And so, it's happened."

I didn't comment because he was right.

I was pretty sure that I had just fallen in love.

CHAPTER 5

Lyrical ~
I was so heated that I couldn't remember walking up the two flights of stairs to the sixth floor.
What assholes.
I mean, I knew that Bruce was a jerk, but for him to let me yell at his lover like that? What bullshit.
I wasn't sure how long I was banging on the door, but after what felt like a million years, it finally swung open. "Holy shit, Lyric," Rena yelped. "Why are you knocking on my door like you're the goddamn police?"
I didn't wait for an invitation into her apartment. I just muscled my way in, and she wisely let me. "I'm going to fucking kill him, Rena," I spat.
Rena shut the door, then watched as I paced her living room. "Kill who?"
"Bruce fucking Higgins," I said, his name like acid on my tongue.
"Okay, calm down," she replied. "Let me get you some tea, so that we can plan his murder calmly and rationally like civilized adults."
I let her head on into the kitchen, then threw myself on her couch. Rena Salinger's been my upstairs neighbor for the entire five years that I'd been living in the building, but she's been my best friend for the past three. Rena and I were the same age at twenty-nine, but she had silky blonde hair and brilliant blue eyes, the complete opposite of me. She was also about five-foot-six with an hourglass figure that I often envied. Her curves weren't exaggerated, but they were very prominent, and she worked those curves like a sexy sex goddess. Rena was also a web designer and worked from home a lot, which was great for me.
Like, right now, for instance.
Rena dropped down on the armchair next to the couch, crossing her legs underneath her butt. "Okay, the tea is a'brewin', so tell me what happened with Bruce."
I grabbed one of the throw pillows on the couch, then lifting it to my face,

I screamed into the poor innocent thing. Once I came up for air, I told her about cussing out Bruce and his lover.

When I was finished, I asked, "And you want to know the worst part of it all?" I didn't wait for her to answer. She was already invested in my story, so of course she wanted to know the worst part of it all. "I actually thought Bruce was hot as hell when I saw him in the lobby, then when we rode up in the elevator together. I mean, Jesus, Rena, talk about a ten."

Rena's brows furrowed as she cocked her head at me. "You actually think Bruce is a *ten?*"

Was she blind?

"Hell, yeah, don't you?" Before she could answer, my mind wandered towards his lover. "But I gotta tell you, Ren, where Bruce is a solid ten, well…probably higher than that, the man did have his shirt off, and…whoa…" Where I'd thought that he'd been stunning fully clothed in the elevator, when I'd gotten a good look at him shirtless, his stunningness had gone up a few notches. "…but his lover? Holy Baby Jesus. His lover was…well, I don't blame him for cheating on Randall with that man."

Rena started shaking her head. "Bruce? You think Bruce is a ten?" she asked again, sounding a bit confused.

However, before I could clarify, the tea kettle-*yes, Rena made her tea the old-fashioned way*-whistled, and she got up to go prepare our drinks. Now, while most people fell victim to coffee, and while I had nothing against it, I preferred tea. It just felt more…soothing. Plus, on cold winter nights, I went with hot chocolate. Nevertheless, I didn't prepare my tea the legit way that Rena did. I heated that shit in the microwave like a true sloth.

Rena returned with our tea, and she still sounded baffled when she placed the cups on the coffee table in the center of her living room. "I…I just never imagined Bruce being your type, Lyric," she said.

I picked up my teacup, then dunked my bag, helping the brewing to come along. "How is gorgeous not my type?" I asked. "Hell, gorgeous is everyone's type."

When I thought back to Bruce's lover, I could feel what a waste the pulsing between my legs was. Why were all the hot men gay or married? Both men were freakin' scorching, so it really was a shame. Especially, when it came to Bruce's lover.

He stood high above me at…I'd say over six-foot, for sure. He had dark chocolate hair, much the same shade as Bruce had. As a matter of fact, now that I thought about it, they rather looked a lot alike. As Mystery Man had stared down at me, I'd seen that his eyes were a bright hazel color with lots of flecks of green that sat below brows matching his hair color. His features were rather Romanesque with a strong, straight nose, sharp cheekbones, and a cut jaw line. His lips were also a soft pink and thick. Plus, he definitely looked like he was built to hold a girl up against the wall with no effort at all.

He had also appeared to be around my age, maybe a couple of years older, but his simple jeans and t-shirt hadn't taken away from how the fabric of his shirt had flowed over muscular planes and grooves, definitely hiding a six-pack underneath all those ridiculous clothes. Plus, he had to be great in the sack for Bruce to risk eviction just to sneak around with him.

"I suppose I just don't think Bruce is gorgeous," Rena said, shrugging a shoulder. "As for cheating on Randall, now that they've been evicted, it makes sense that Bruce wouldn't care who helped him get the rest of his stuff."

The tea burned my tongue.

"What?"

Did she just say…

She grinned, holding her cup close to her face. "So, on Wednesday, there was all kinds of commotion in the building, and I found out from Sally Ruth that the owner of the building had somehow found out about Randall and Bruce, so he came over, fired Randall, then evicted them both."

My eyes widened, my burnt tongue forgotten. "What? How…why didn't you call me or text me or something?"

Rena took a sip of her tea before setting it down. "Because you were away at work," she replied. "I didn't want to bother you."

Was she for real?

This kind of news was worth being bothered for. "Holy shit," I exclaimed. "This has got to be the best news ever."

"See? So, their murder is no longer necessary," she reasoned. "Still, I'm surprised to hear Bruce was still cleaning out his apartment. The rumors I heard were that both he and Randall had been banned from the property."

Wow…this was big.

This meant sleep; sweet, restful, blessed sleep.

"Well, maybe now that Randall can't do anything for him, Bruce has moved on to the new guy," I said, suddenly feeling a little bit sorry for Randall.

"I still can't believe you think Bruce is a ten," she repeated. "I mean, I obviously have nothing against blondes, I just didn't think they did it for you."

Blondes?

I set my tea down, then curled my legs underneath my ass. "Blonde?"

Rena cocked her head, looking a bit puzzled, but then her eyes widened. "Lyrical, Bruce is blonde," she drawled out slowly.

I shook my head in denial. "No, he's not," I argued. "He's tall with brown hair and hazel eyes."

I thought back to that day when I'd seen him and Randall kissing through the crack in his door, and admittedly, I had mostly seen Randall cradling another man. By that time, I had hated him so much that I hadn't paid attention to the details.

Rena was shaking her head at me. "No, he's not," she argued back. "He's only like five-eleven and is blonder than I am."

I wanted to continue argueing with her, but since I'd never actually met Bruce until now-*maybe*-it was hard to dispute her claims. In order to preserve my God-given freedom, I'd made great efforts to avoid Bruce in the weeks that he'd been living here. Yet now…

"Then who the hell was in his apartment hammering at shit?" However, even as I said the words, a cold dread settled in the pit of my stomach. "Contractors?" I asked in a hopeful voice.

Rena's lips curled in, and she looked sorry for me. "Okay. I'm going to just ask," she said, straightening her back, steeling herself for some great revelation. "Did the two men you cussed out *both* have brown hair and hazel eyes? Did they look alike? And did they *both* look like you could probably orgasm from just looking at them?"

My heart started beating faster, and I could feel goosebumps break out all over my body. My mouth that housed my burnt tongue wouldn't work, and I suddenly had an image of me sitting on a park bench, all my belongings in a trash bag next to me. As that picture depressed the hell out of me, I stared at my friend as I nodded my confirmation of her apt description of the two gods that I had just cussed out in spectacular fashion.

"Oh, Lyrical," she mumbled. "You didn't cuss out Bruce and his secret lover." Even before she said the words, I knew this was bad. "Mind you, I haven't seen them, but according to Sally Ruth, the two men you just verbally assaulted were Nixon St. James, the owner of this building, and his brother, Lincoln St. James, who also happens to be his lawyer."

"What?" I squeaked, my voice barely above a whisper.

This couldn't be.

There was no way that I could have made this huge of a mistake.

Rena nodded her head. "According to Sally Ruth, Mr. St. James decided to clean up the mess that Bruce left behind himself and recruited his brother to help, but that's all I know."

Now, stop!

This was the part where you might want to look for the nearest window, then jump to your death. However, on the off chance that you survived, suicide was an actual crime. So, just don't.

Do. Not.

At least, not today.

CHAPTER 6

Nixon ~
Lyrical Rodgers.
What a hell of a name.
    I wondered if her parents were hippies or something like that. I mean, my brothers' and my names weren't too common, but I couldn't think if I'd ever heard the name Lyrical before.
    After she had stormed off-without a bra or shoes-it'd taken everything that I'd had to finish up the repairs that Linc and I had been working on. It'd taken us well into the evening before we'd been finished with everything, but we'd gotten it all done. Unfortunately, we'd left the building without another Lyrical sighting, and, boy, did I want to see her again.
    It hadn't helped that Lincoln wouldn't shut up about how she'd thought that he was sexy. I had managed to stow away my irritation by telling myself that, if she thought that Lincoln was sexy, then she had to think that I was sexy by default since we looked alike. Hell, all of us looked just like our dad, except that Jackson had gotten Mom's blue eyes, instead of Dad's hazel ones. However, other than that, we all looked similar. So, if she thought that Lincoln was sexy...well, then, I was also sexy, and so was Jackson.
    Plus, as if my obsession with Lyrical wasn't bad enough, the second that I'd made it home, I had headed straight into my office, pulled up the Canal rental property, then had broken the motherfucking law. I had pulled up Lyrical's rental agreement information to stalk her.
    However, I hadn't been irresponsible about my stalking. Before powering up my computer, I had called Lincoln, then asked him just how illegal was I about to get. He'd told me that invasion of personal privacy was a pretty big deal, to which I had ignored, then hung up on him.
    So, armed with Lyrical's name, I had cyber-stalked all her social media sites. After a couple of hours, I had managed to find out that she worked as a pet store manager, had one sister, both her parents were alive and well, and she had a best friend that also lived in the Canal building.

Most importantly, I had been able to deduce from her online presence that she wasn't married, nor did she have a boyfriend. I also noted that most of her friends called her Lyric, and I found that I liked both versions of her unique name.

Now it was Sunday evening, and still seated at my desk, my eyes glued to the computer screen, it dawned on me just how frightening it was to realize just how easily someone could pick apart your life if they knew just where to look on the internet.

As I was comparing my stalking skills to those of others, my phone rang. I grabbed it off my desk, then saw that it was Jackson, so I answered, of course. "What's up?"

"Hey, Nix," he replied easily, and I smiled.

Though understandable, Jackson was way too serious sometimes. I got that his job was stressful, and that he was super dedicated to it, but he needed to find a way to enjoy the rest of his life, too. Granted, Linc and I also took our jobs seriously, but we weren't absorbed by our careers the way that Jackson was. He seemed to only be happy when he was tending to his patients.

It was also kind of funny how my brothers were perceived. Lincoln was so easy-going that you'd never guess that he was a ruthless criminal defense attorney. Seriously, watching him in action in the courtroom was such a contrast to his personality outside of it. Granted, when you had people's freedom in the palm of your hand, then you had to always give more than your all, and Linc always delivered on his promises to his clients.

Jackson was also a bit of an enigma. He was one of the best pediatric physicians in the state, but looking at him, you'd have your doubts. His dimples were reserved for his patients only…well, his patients and his family, but everyone else got the serious doctor. Colleagues, co-workers, patients' parents, hospital staff, and the rest of the world…well, they were all greeted with a six-foot-two, tattooed mass of muscle, seriousness, and unparalleled medical talent.

My eldest brother also made no effort to hide his tattoos or his scowl. However, his medical reputation and the bond that he created with his patients was enough that no one minded the tattoos or the scowl. The second that a parent saw Jackson with their child, all preconceived notions of my brother's abilities became non-existent.

"To what do I owe the honor," I joked.

I could hear Jackson huff over the phone. "You still making it to dinner on Wednesday?"

Once a month, our mother insisted on a family dinner. While she was very proud of us, she was adamant that our careers were not going to come before family. So, once a month, we had to clear an evening on our calendars for a family get-together. Jackson's only exception was if he got an emergency call during dinner, then he was allowed to leave.

"Yeah," I answered. "I'll be there."

My brother chuckled. "It's not like we really have a choice."

He wasn't wrong.

"Not unless you want Dad kicking your ass for upsetting his wife," I pointed out. "I'm not trying to get my ass kicked, Jackson."

Jackson let out a small laugh. "I'd rather Dad kick my ass than watch Mom cry," he countered.

I winced. No one wanted to see Mom cry. Mom was our hero. She was the St. James' men's sole purpose for existing. "No shit," I grimaced.

"Anyway," he said, pulling me away from the image of Mom crying, "the reason I called was to give you a heads up."

"Jesus," I murmured. "What'd Linc do now?"

Jackson laughed. "Nothing. Well, nothing that I know of," he amended. "This isn't about Linc. I just wanted to warn you that when I was helping Mom buy some more flowers for her garden yesterday, we ran into Dina Rivers at Healthy Gardens. As I stood there-my ears bleeding everywhere-she was catching up with Mom and telling Mom how she's divorced, and how she moved back to town for a fresh start."

"So?" I had no idea what Dina Rivers had to do with me.

I could hear Jackson sigh over the phone. *"So?"* he parroted.

"Yeah. So?" I repeated. "What's Dina have to do with me?"

"Jesus, Nix," he grumbled. "I don't know how you can have the brain of a financial wizard but be so dense. You dated the girl for four months. You don't think she was hinting at Mom about her fresh start?"

"Uh, first off, I didn't *date* Dina for four months. We hooked up when our schedules lined up," I corrected. "Second, I have no desire to pick up from where we left off."

"I got news for you, little brother," Jackson retorted. "You might have been only hooking up with her, but she was *dating* you. Besides, why would you introduce someone you were just hooking up with to your family?"

He was right; I would *never* introduce my family to someone that I was just fucking. However...

"I didn't *introduce* her to you guys willingly. That one time she met you and Linc, she made an unannounced appearance at my office. And the one time she met Mom and Dad, they showed up early for our lunch date, and Dina was still at my place," I reminded him. "I might be a dick, but I'm not such an asshole that I'm not going to make proper introductions when the woman still had my handprints on her ass, Jackson."

Jackson chuckled again. "Jesus, you're something else."

"Look," I told him. "It's fine. Whatever Dina is doing has nothing to do with me, Jackson. I'm sorry to hear about her divorce, but it's been, what...a least a year since I've seen her, and longer than that since I've been with her. I'm sure she was just making polite conversation. Honestly, I haven't given Dina Rivers a thought since the last time I did speak with her."

"All right," he conceded. "If you say so, Nix. Just don't say I didn't warn you when you come home to a bunny boiling on your stovetop."

I laughed. Dina Rivers might have had bigger plans for us than I'd had, but I didn't think that she was a full-blown psychopath. "Jackson, even *my* ego's not so big that I think Dina's been carrying a torch for me all this time."

"True. You are kind of a dick," he agreed. "Now that I think about it, you're probably right."

"Says the man who has an aversion to smiling," I snorted.

"Hey," he scoffed. "I smile all the time."

"Yeah, but only to people under the age of eighteen," I pointed out.

"They're the only people worth smiling at," Jackson retorted.

I laughed because he wasn't entirely wrong. "Well, I appreciate the call, but I got some online stalking to get to."

For a man not prone to smiling, I knew that he was smiling now. "Oh, yeah," he chuckled. "Lincoln told me all about the hot brunette who handed you your gay ass the other day."

I rolled my eyes. "Did your brother also tell you how he encouraged her gay opinion of me?"

Jackson laughed. "He sure did," he replied. "You know Linc, he never leaves anything out. He's all about the details."

"Yeah, well, I need to do a little more recon before asking her out," I added, ignoring his observations on Lincoln.

"And that's the reason I don't date," Jackson snorted. "Things sure are different from the days when you could just approach a woman and ask her out to dinner."

I scoffed at that. "You don't date because you're a bigger asshole than I am."

"At least, I'm not a stalker," he countered.

"Yet," I volleyed. "Wait until you meet a sassy brunette who turns you stupid."

CHAPTER 7

Lyrical ~
"So, I might have to move back home and live off your good graces and occasional handouts for a while," I announced.

Now, stop!

This was a family dinner where you might not want to air your dirty laundry in front of your perfect sister and hardworking parents. You know, that family dinner where your parents doted on the perfect sibling, and you just wanted to stab everyone with your fork, but assault with the intent to commit bodily harm came with *real* jail time, so you just gritted your teeth and tried not to choke on your steamed peas?

Well, thankfully, I didn't have that kind of judgmental family, so I'd always felt safe announcing my failures for my sister and parents to join in on the excitement.

"Why? What happened?" my sister asked.

I pointed my fork that was filled with a heap of mashed potatoes at her. "In my defense, I hadn't slept in weeks," I started, then amended, "Well, except for the two nights prior, but still..."

My father sighed. "Lyric, you don't have to defend yourself to us," he reminded me.

If there was one thing that I could say about Janice and Louis Rodgers, it was that they were truly the stone-cold definition of supportive parents. When my parents say that they just want me and Alice to be happy, they mean just that.

"So, what happened?" Alice asked again.

I swallowed my bite of mashed potatoes, then steeled myself for the laughter that was sure to come. "It was a case of mistaken identity," I began. "Last Friday afternoon, after I got back from St. Louis, I mistook my building manager, Nixon St. James, for the rude neighbor that I've been telling you guys about, and I may, or may not, have cussed him out."

My mother's fork stopped midway to her mouth. "You used actual curse words, or is this situation salvageable?"

"I used actual curse words, accused him of cheating on his gay lover with his own brother, and then accused him of not being gay, but being so opportunistic that he'd pretend to be gay just to score a come up," I confessed.

My mother's fork went into her mouth, my father took a drink of his beer, and my sister's fork clattered against her dinner plate.

Five…four…three….

Alice erupted first, and once her laughter flowed over the table, my mom and dad joined in like assholes.

"Okay, you jerks," I scowled. "Laugh it up. But you won't be laughing when you have your twenty-nine-year-old daughter living back home with you and disrupting how you guys get down at night."

My dad was the first person to get himself under control. "Okay, okay," he said, still chuckling. "We're sorry, Lyric. We didn't mean to laugh at you-"

"Yes. Yes, you did," I argued, narrowing my eyes at him.

My dad smiled, and it was like looking in a mirror. I'd taken after my dad in looks while Alice had taken after our mother. I had Dad's brown hair, brown eyes, and smile. Alice had Mom's auburn hair, blue eyes, and damn near my mom's entire face, and both women were extremely beautiful.

"Can you blame us?" he asked sheepishly.

"A little support here," I harrumphed.

My mom slapped a hand at me. "Oh, Lyrical," she chuckled. "You know we support you. And if you do get evicted, you can always take your old room back."

Alice finally settled down. "So, he's not gay or into incest?"

This time, I narrowed my eyes at my sister. "No," I clipped. "He's not gay. He made that very clear when he was trying to defend himself, and I'm pretty sure he's not into his own brother." I shrugged my shoulders. "But people, ya know? You never know what goes on behind closed doors."

Alice just smiled my mom's smile while my dad chimed in, "I seriously don't think you can legally be evicted for cussing out the property owner, Lyric. At least, I don't think so."

"Your father's right, honey," my mom added. "As long as you have a good standing history of paying your rent on time and not causing any issues, you should be fine."

"Okay. Well, then do you guys have any advice on mortification?" I asked. "Because let me tell you, if I never see that man again, it'll be too soon."

"Oh, come on, Lyric. It couldn't have been that bad," my sister said, trying to put a positive spin on the debacle. "I mean, if it was, he'd have evicted you by now, wouldn't he have?"

I shrugged a shoulder. "I don't know. I've never been evicted before, so I'm not sure how it works," I said right before I shoved a piece of steak in my mouth. I was definitely eating my feelings this evening.

"I'm sure if you just apologize and explain, he'll understand," my father said, trying to help.

I thought about that, and I seriously wondered if my pity party wasn't due more to the fact that I had embarrassed myself beyond what I usually did. Now, for the most part, I very rarely cared what people thought of me. I had learned long ago that people were going to judge you for being too perfect just as harshly as they'd judge you for being a loser. So, I lived my life investing in my happiness, but I also did my best not to be a total dick to the people around me. However, sometimes the lines got murky because I had a tendency to speak my mind. I didn't like lying, and I'd rather remain silent than engage in little white lies. Unfortunately, my silence came off as rude sometimes, but I didn't mean to be rude at all.

I stabbed at my steak. "I don't want to apologize," I grumbled. "I hope I never see either of them ever again."

"Lyric," my mother began, "while I understand how embarrassing this must be for you, apologizing to those men is the right thing to do."

I looked up at my mother. "I accused him of being a fake gay hustler that had no shame about cheating on his latest mark with his own brother, Janice," I reiterated. "I'm beyond embarrassed."

"Do not call your mother Janice," my dad chastised.

I rolled my eyes. "Sorry, Mom," I grumbled. "But this is mortification at its finest."

I could see my mom was about to say something, but then her mom's eyes flew over to my sister. "Alice, what on earth are you doing?" she asked. "You know there are no phones allowed at the table during our family dinners."

Alice smiled as she held up her phone, then shoved it in my mother's face. "This is why she's embarrassed."

Unfortunately for me, the kitchen table was a small rectangular table that was big enough to fit only six people. Now, in most normal settings, my father would sit at the head of the table with my mom opposite him, then me and Alice on either side, facing each other. However, we weren't traditionalists like that. If we were, then my name wouldn't be Lyrical.

So, my dad and mother sat sitting next to each other, opposite Alice and me, the chairs on either end of the table sat unused. So, since Alice was sitting directly opposite Mom, she was able to see exactly what Alice had pulled up on her phone.

"Oh, my," my mother fluttered.

"What's that?" my dad asked.

My mom's eyebrows shot upward. "I can see why Lyric's a bit…ruffled…"

Curious, my dad's eyes scanned Alice's phone really quickly, but then he just rolled his eyes and got back to eating. Still, I could see the small smile touching the corner of his lips.

"What is that?" I asked. "What's she showing you?"

Alice turned to face me, and with her phone all up in my face, I could see what she was displaying on her phone. She had looked up Nixon St. James, and there, in full living color, was a picture of the man.

Fuck my life.

Facing back to my plate of food, I shrugged a shoulder, then tried to act all unaffected like. "So, the man looks decent. Who cares?"

Alice gasped. "Looks decent?" she exclaimed. "Are you blind? That is *not* looks decent, Lyric. That's hot as hell."

"Hey," my father muttered, trying his best to curb the hot guy talk.

Alice looked over at Dad. "Sorry, Dad," she said sweetly. "But there's no denying that Nixon St. James is the stuff of fantasies. Just ask your wife."

"I have no idea of what you speak, Alice," my mother lied. "There is no man more stunning on this planet than your father."

My father laughed while Alice and I chuckled.

God, I loved my family.

My father pinned me with a stare. "See, Lyrical. Since I'm the most handsomest man on the planet, you have no cause to be embarrassed in front of any other man."

My heart melted a little as I smiled. "Thanks, Dad."

He smiled back. "Nothing is ever as bad as our insecurities make it out to be," he said wisely.

He was right, and even without his sage advice, I knew that I was going to have to get over it. I was about to reassure him when Alice's voice cut through the room.

"Oh, shit," she rushed out. "He has *two* brothers."

CHAPTER 8

Nixon ~
"So, I hear that we're finally going to get a daughter-in-law," my mother announced not two seconds after we were all seated around the table.

We were sitting in the formal dining room, and I was pretty sure that this was the only time that my parents ever used this room. If it wasn't Easter, Christmas, or this mandatory monthly dinner, my parents usually just ate at the kitchen table.

Jackson St. James Sr. was a retired judge, and Felicia St. James was a retired family attorney. So, with good, solid, long-standing careers behind them, they were able to afford the finer things in life, and their home was one of those finer things. However, their house wasn't big or obnoxious. On the contrary, it was a quaint two-story, four-bedroom home. It was the inside that made it classy because my parent's home was furnished in good taste. Thankfully, it was still livable; no need to take off your shoes before entering.

Now, between both my parents, they were a walking, talking, living law library, and while Lincoln had taken after them profession-wise, my parents had never pushed us one way or another in choosing a career. They hadn't been heartbroken when Jackson had said that he'd wanted to be a doctor, or when I'd said that I wanted to be an architect. They also hadn't celebrated the house down when Linc had said he wanted to be a lawyer. Our parents just wanted us all to be happy, and if we were happy, then that was enough for them.

Now, while this dinner took place in the formal dining room, we were still anything but. Casual clothes were worn everywhere, and curse words were only banned out of respect for my mother. Dad was the only one allowed to cuss.

"Jesus," I mumbled, placing a napkin over my lap. It was a paper napkin because my mother thought that cloth napkins were ridiculous and useless. "Is there nothing sacred in this family?"

"Nope," Linc answered.

"Not at all," Jackson added.

"Not since the day you were born," my dad threw in right before he took a sip of his wine.

"Don't be ridiculous," my mom chided.

My father set his glass of wine down, then speared me with a look. "Have you made it clear to the young lady that you're not gay?"

Jesus.

There really was nothing sacred in this family.

I cocked my head at the man. "I haven't even seen her since Friday, Dad," I answered. "Now, can we just eat a nice dinner without talking about Lyrical?"

"Lyrical?" my mother echoed. "Oh, my…is that my future daughter-in-law's name?"

I could feel my eyes bugging out of my head. "Mom," I said, steadying my breathing.

Her chocolate brows shot upward. "What?"

Weirdos.

All of them.

Still, it was hard to be stern with my mother. She was all of five-foot-two, and with the exception of Jackson getting her blue eyes, none of us looked like her. She had light brown hair, bright blue eyes, and her petite frame made us want to exist for nothing but protecting her and making her happy.

Mom was also all femininity while my father was all masculinity. Dad was strong, fair, and solid, and he had raised us to be the same. His only weakness was our only weakness, and that was Mom.

I went to cutting my rib-eye, wishing we could talk about anything else but knowing better. However, before I could answer her, Jackson decided to take the wheel. "Yeah, that's her name," he said, answering her. "Nixon's been stalking her the past few days, so he ought to know."

"Oh, that is such a beautifully unique name," she said, not caring how ludicrous this topic was, or that I was committing the crime of stalking.

"She's smokin' hot, too," Linc decided to add.

I shot him a look. "Do you mind?" Then looking back at my mother, I asked, "Why can't we talk about the ladies that Lincoln or Jackson are interested in?"

My dad snorted. "Is that what you call them? Ladies?"

"Jackson," my mother hissed. "Be nice."

Dad looked across the table at my mother. "Seriously, Felicia?" he retorted. "Since when has Lincoln or Jackson ever brought home a nice lady for us to meet? Or Nixon, for that matter?"

"Hey," Jackson objected. "Just because I'm not looking for a serious relationship doesn't mean that the women that I meet occupy street corners, Dad."

Simultaneously, we all turned to look at Linc. His fork stopped midway to his mouth as his eyes scanned our faces. "Oh, hey," he yelped. "I've never picked up a hooker."

My mother shook her head, no doubt wanting to rid herself of the picture of her second born pulling up to a street corner. "At any rate, I'm not interested in Jackson's flavor of the month or Lincoln's flavor of the week-"

"Day," I corrected.

"Hour," Jackson added.

"Suck my-"

"Hey!" Dad boomed, cutting Lincoln off. "There will be no talk of dick sucking at the dinner table."

Jackson looked over at Dad. "So, the topic's fair game as long as we're not eating dinner?" he asked sardonically.

"Watch it, Jackson," my father muttered. "I can still kick your ass."

"Not without Mom's help," my brother snorted.

"Can we please get back to Nixon's girlfriend?" my mother asked, ending all other conversations.

Luckily, I was done swallowing my food, or else I probably would have choked on it. "Mom, Lyrical is *not* my girlfriend," I clarified again. "I've only spoken to her that one time, and as I'm sure Lincoln didn't spare any details in his gossip-fest, that one time didn't go all that well."

"She thinks I'm sexy," Lincoln threw in for good measure.

I sliced my brother with a look as my mother cooed, "Well, of course, she thinks you're sexy. My boys are all handsome."

"How soon before we get grandchildren?" my father questioned, eyeing me over his fork full of broccoli. "We're not getting any younger, you know."

"Jesus Christ, Dad," I replied, surprised but not surprised. I mean, it wasn't like I hadn't known these people all my life. "We haven't even been on a date yet. Can you give me a little more time here?"

"A surprise pregnancy, how wonderful," my mother exclaimed, a smile beaming across her beautiful face.

I looked at my parents-*who just happened to be the epitome of law and order*-and wondered how they became so stunted. Maybe it was their retirement. Like, if you didn't stimulate your brain anymore, weird shit started taking up residence in your head. I was going to have to look up hobbies for my golden years because I didn't want to end up a wacko like these two.

"No one is getting pregnant, Mom," I told her. "Can I just work on getting a first date first?" I looked between my parents. "I promise to work on the unplanned pregnancy and shotgun wedding afterwards, but just…give me some time."

My mom huffed, then went back to cutting another piece of her steak. "I don't see what the big deal is," she muttered. "Any girl should be happy to be knocked up by any of you sweet boys."

Jackson reached up, then pinched his nose. Clearly, he saw that our parents were losing their minds just like I did. "Mom…" he said calmly, but then he must have thought better of it because he just trailed off and didn't say anything more.

"Sorry, Mom," Linc chimed in. "No unplanned pregnancies here. I'm super responsible."

I glared at my brother. "This is all your fault, Linc," I accused. "All you had to do was keep your goddamn mouth shut."

"Language," my father growled.

"Puhleeeeeeeease," he remarked. "There's no way I was going to be able to keep that shit to myself."

"Language," my father repeated.

"I mean, Christ, Nix," Linc said, ignoring our father. "She stormed in, accused you of being gay, then accused you of not being gay, then accused you of cheating on your gay lover with me. How in the hell did you expect me to keep that shit to myself?"

"He's got a point," Jackson quipped, not looking up from his plate of food.

My father's fist banged on the table. "Goddamn it, you two!" he thundered. "Language! Quit fucking cursing around your mother!"

We all stopped, then looked over at Dad.

"Thank you, Jackson," Mom whispered sweetly, causing me to roll my eyes at her clear signs of insanity. "I love you, honey."

"I love you, too, Sheesh," he grumbled, using his nickname for my mother.

My eyes bounced back and forth between every member of my family as I wondered how we didn't have a circus named after us by now.

I also wondered how soon was too soon to get a certain psychotic brunette pregnant.

CHAPTER 9

Lyrical ~
Whoever said that being a ninja wasn't hard obviously hadn't ever tried being a ninja. Seriously, adopting the skill of stealth was a hard sonofabitch.

Like a coward, I had spent the last few days coming and going from my apartment through back and side entrances to avoid any chance of the possibility of running into Nixon St. James or that jackass brother of his. Ugh, I still couldn't believe that I thought that the man was sexy. I mean, sure he was hot as hell; they both were. Still, I didn't have to like it.

Then holy six-pack Batman, when Alice had pulled up a picture of all the St. James men, I'd had to get an extra napkin to wipe the drool off my face. Why did The Lord do that? I mean, wasn't there a standard in a family where you had one hot brother, one nerdy brother, and one ugly brother? Didn't they have to balance the universe out? Why would God create three-*count them, THREE*-absolute male perfections and put them all in the same family? I bet the dad was hot, too.

Meanwhile, over here in Rodgers Land, Alice had stunning auburn hair, fierce green eyes, and was slim, but feminine. However, me? I was shaped like a pear. I was shaped like the fruit that was left lonely in the fruit bowl after everyone's eaten the apples, oranges, bananas, and nectarines. It was straight up bullshit if you asked me.

Also, because it wasn't enough that I was as sexy as a pear, I'd had to go and humiliate myself in front of, not one, but *two* sex gods, and now I had to live the rest of my life hiding in shadows and trying to blend in with the homeless.

Yeah, I could move back home, but I wasn't too eager to hear my parents going at it at night any more than they were eager to have to keep it down because I could hear them going at it. So, I had decided that I wasn't going to move unless Mr. St. James really did evict me.

God, I hope that he didn't evict me.

"You're not going to be evicted, Lyric," Rena said, echoing my thoughts.

I looked up at her from where I was sitting on the couch. "You can't know that for sure," I argued.

It was Friday night, one week after the 'incident', and we were vegging out in my apartment, drinking this shitastic week away. Sure, things were great at work, but trying to break in and out of your own home, unseen, took a lot of damn work, and it was exhausting as hell.

"Lyric, it's been a week," she reasoned. "I'm sure you would have gotten a notice or something by now, don't you think?"

"Maybe," I conceded, though still not entirely positive.

Nevertheless, I needed to come up with a better plan than becoming a ninja. My paranoia was the reason that we were staying in and drinking tonight, instead of heading out to a club and getting drunk enough to jump a random stranger. I was afraid that in my inebriated state, I would forget my ninja commitments, then accidently show myself out in the open for Mr. St. James to pounce on.

Granted, my nether regions weren't objecting to his possible pouncing, but I didn't think that my mind and body were on the same pouncing page.

Rena sat down next to me, handing me a shot of tequila. "Why don't you just bite the bullet and go talk with him? Clear the air," she suggested.

Now, stop!

While her suggestion might have merit, I wasn't sure if he'd agree to an appointment to speak with me after everything that I accused him of. So, then that would mean that I'd have to show up at his office unannounced, and depending on how my arrival was embraced, my mind was conjuring up all kinds of images of me running from his security until I was caught by the actual law, and then being charged with trespassing and running from the police, and believe you me, you did not want to go down that road. Trespassing charges could lead to restraining orders, and that shit stayed on your record forever. So, for the rest of your life, you were going to have to explain how your crazy actually reached the level to warrant a restraining order.

Not the best plan.

"My dad suggested the same thing, but why voluntarily throw myself in front of a bullet, ya know," I muttered.

We threw back our shots before Rena replied, "How long do you think you'll be able to be a ninja, Lyric? I mean, I think you're doing a fantastic job so far, but sooner or later, you're going to have to interact with the real world."

"Maybe I can just send him an apology card?" I suggested, and the more I thought about it, the more the idea had merit. "I mean, it's an apology without throwing myself in front of the bullet, yeah?"

Rena took a drink of her beer, her face pensive like she was really giving it some thought. "A card might work," she agreed, then her eyes found mine, and her face brightened up like Christmas morning. "Or you can show up at his office, naked with only a trench coat, and *really* apologize."

I snorted. "If I had your body, that might work. But I just can't see a man who looks like that attracted to pears."

Rena narrowed her eyes at me. "I hate when you do that," she said sternly. "You are absolutely beautiful with a great body, Lyric. I've seen the way men check you out when you walk by."

I chuckled. "That's because they're probably wondering if the jiggle in my ass ever comes to a complete stop." The direction of this conversation required a heavy pull of my beer.

"You have a sexy body," Rena argued. "Men love a nice, thick, plumped ass."

My eyes scanned her body. "No. Men like a Jessica Rabbit body," I countered.

Rena shook her head. "I think we're both wrong," she replied. "I think men like pussy, period. I don't think they really care what the package around it looks like."

If only that were true.

"Have you gone online to stalk them yet?" I asked. "Because if you have, you'll see that those men can get any woman they want. Even if your theory was correct, I repeat, they can get *any* woman they want."

Rena cocked her head before jumping out of her chair like a goddamn lunatic. "More shots!"

I shook my head, wondering why that girl was single. Rena was beautiful, smart, sassy, and full of moxie, and I'd totally date her if I swung that way.

When she returned with our fourth shot of the evening, hers was already making its way down her esophagus before her ass had even hit the chair cushions. I threw back my shot, and the second that my head came back down, I knew that I had just crossed over from buzzed to legally intoxicated.

"So," Rena said, bringing me out of my self-realization, "I *have* stalked the St. James brothers on the internet, and I gotta ask, Lyric. Would you jump Nixon's bones if he was interested?"

Even without the beers and shots of liquor, that was an easy question to answer. "Hell, yeah, I'd jump his bones," I retorted. "I mean, that'd be like a crime against humanity not to take a man who looks like that up on an offer of wild sex."

Rena started laughing like a loon, and it looked like I wasn't on this side of intoxicated alone. "Oh, my God," she exclaimed. "How awful would it be if he had a small dick?"

My eyes almost bugged out of my head. *"Don't say that."* I mean, what a horrible jinx. Men that looked as good as the St. James brothers but had small dicks was Satan's work.

Rena wasn't fazed. "What?" she asked. "It's been known to happen, you know."

I shook my head, trying to rid myself of that abomination of a thought. "Well, if I'm fortunate enough to ever get his penis, instead of an eviction notice, then I'll let you know the size of his manhood. However, I'm still leaning towards getting evicted."

Rena's head dropped back onto the back of the chair. "I bet you guys would make beautiful babies," she murmured.

I snorted. "That man is not looking to have babies with me," I told her, killing her dreams. "Ugh, why couldn't I like his brother?"

Rena's head popped back up. "You did say the man was sexy," she reminded me.

"He was…*is*," I amended. "But once I got a look at Nixon…Holy Mary, Mother of God," I sighed dramatically. "My lady bits had ignored Lincoln and focused all their lustful attention on Nixon. Stupid lady bits," I mumbled.

Before Rena could comment on my lady bits and how stupid they were, there was a knock at the door. "I'll get it," she sing-songed as she got up to go check who could be knocking on my door on a Friday night.

As I thought about it, the only person that I could think that it could be was Alice. However, Alice had a life, so why would she be knocking at my door on a Friday night? I heard Rena open the door, but I didn't bother to look to see who it was, and that was my first mistake of the night.

Seriously.

"Uh…" Rena's voice trailed off, but then she said, "Lyric, someone's at the door for you."

"Did they bring more alcohol?" I called, not moving from the couch.

Then my eyes closed in absolute mortification as my lady bits became stupider when a deep, rough, masculine voice that I'd heard before reached my ears. "No," he said. "I didn't bring any alcohol. I just brought me."

My head whipped around so fast that it would have done The Exorcist proud. My eyes rounded as I briefly wondered what Rena had put in those shots, my eyes staring into the perfect face of Nixon St. James.

What. In. The. Hell?

CHAPTER 10

Nixon ~
I usually cursed people that kept their faces glued to their phones, but this was one of those moments where I wish that I'd had my phone out; Lyrical's face looked priceless.

I also noticed that her eyes were a little bloodshot, and that made her request for alcohol make more sense.

She leaped off the couch-*more gracefully than I would have expected*-then just stood there, staring at me. After a few seconds, she spoke, and I wondered just how drunk she was. "I thought the sheriff would show up. What are you doing here?"

My brows furrowed as I cocked my head. "The sheriff?"

Lyrical rolled her eyes. "Yeah," she said, all duh-like. "You know, the sheriff?"

"I don't know him personally, but I do know what a sheriff is," I replied, not knowing at all why she was expecting the sheriff. I mean, what kind of party were these two having?

"Uh, I think I'll just...uh..."

Lyrical was around the couch, then standing in front of her friend quicker than I thought her capable. "You will just not just nothing," she hissed, then she got on her tiptoes to look her friend in the eye. "You better not leave me."

Then God bless drunk friends.

It took everything that I had not to flat out laugh the place down when her friend whispered-not whispered, "I have to leave, Lyric. How else are you going to jump him if I stay?"

Lyrical's gasp was Broadway-worthy, and I was actually surprised that she hadn't tipped over in her outrage. *"Rena."*

I stuck my hand out towards the blonde. "Hi, Rena," I said. "I'm Nixon. It's nice to meet you."

Rena took my hand in hers-completely ignoring an outraged Lyrical-and said, "Hi, Nixon. It's nice to meet you, too."

Lyrical reached out, then snatched Rena's hand out of mine. "Oh, my God," she screeched. "What kind of best friend are you, consorting with the enemy like that?"

The enemy?

With that, the odds of me scoring a date with Lyrical just plummeted. How was I going to tell my mom and dad that their dreams of an unplanned pregnancy and shotgun wedding were not going to come true?

"The enemy?" I asked, trying to see if it was the alcohol talking or just her crazy mind at work.

Lyrical turned towards me. "Well, of course, you're the enemy," she replied. "Why wouldn't you be?"

I stuck my hands in my pockets to keep from reaching for her, then just kissing the hell out of her. "Why would I be?"

"Uh, so...yeah, I'm just-"

"You leave, and you are dead to me, Rena," she threatened as she turned back to face her friend. "Dead. Like deader than dead. Not fake dead."

"What's fake dead?" I asked, because...how could I not?

Turning back to me, Lyrical narrowed her eyes. "Fake dead is when you fake being dead, Nixon. Jesus," she mumbled, exasperated.

I couldn't make heads or tails of that sentence, but I did know one thing.

She had used my first name.

It had also fallen off her lips like we'd known each other for years.

Before I could garner up a reply, Lyrical planted her hands on her hips as she glared up at me. "What are you doing here? Are you here to evict me?"

I had to admit, most of the things that she'd said since I'd met her had been full of surprises, but this was the biggest. I shook my head. "No," I answered. "Why would you think I'd evict you?"

She cocked her head, then looked at me like I was the dumbest motherfucker on the planet. "Why would you evict me?" she parroted. "Oh, I don't know. Maybe the fact that I cussed you out for being a straight man pretending to be a gay man just to come up on a hustle? I mean, why else would you be here?"

I couldn't help the smirk that hit my lips. "I'm here to prove to you that I'm not gay," I answered honestly, and Rena gasped as Lyrical's eyes rounded to the size of dinner plates.

Christ, she had beautiful eyes.

"Fuck this," Rena rushed out. "I'm leaving." Then she ran out the door before either of us could stop her or encourage her.

"Wha...yo...how...what...*what?*" Lyric sputtered as the door shut behind Rena.

Armed with her friend's slip of the tongue, I stepped to her until she had to tilt her head back to look at me. "I *said* that I'm here to prove to you that

I'm not gay," I repeated. "I'm also here to prove that I'm not straight pretending to be gay or cheating on my lover with my brother."

Lyrical's eyes went from dinner plates to narrowed little slits. "Are you seriously daring to come into *my* home and make fun of me?" she asked menacingly.

I smirked again. I couldn't help it. This woman was fucking fascinating. "No," I answered. "I'm here to ask you to have dinner with me."

I wasn't sure if it was the alcohol or her lack of restraint, but she looked genuinely bewildered when she screeched, "Why on earth would you want to go to dinner with *me*?"

This time, *I* narrowed my eyes at *her*. "Why wouldn't I?"

Stepping back on her left foot, she leaned back as her eyes raked down my body before meeting back up with my eyes. "Look at *you*," she drawled out dramatically. "I mean, Christ on a pogo stick, you could be having dinner with any woman on the planet."

Any woman on the planet was stretching it a bit. I mean, I knew that I wasn't a bad-looking guy, but any woman on the planet? That was insinuating that I could have my pick of any lesbian out there, and that my looks were enough to switch which team she batted for, and that simply wasn't true.

"Even lesbians?" I asked just to trip her up.

Her energy evaporated just like that. "Well, of course, *not* lesbians, you dolt."

Dolt?

"Then you're exaggerating," I pointed out.

She slapped her hands on her hips as she corrected herself. "Fine. Any *straight* woman," she amended.

"Even married ones?" I asked just to be contrary. I knew what she was getting at, but it was just so damn much fun fucking with her.

However, instead of volleying verbally back, she narrowed her eyes at me again, then said, "Get out of my house."

I shook my head. "Not until you agree to have dinner with me," I replied.

"Why?" she asked again, looking genuinely confused. Or maybe she was just that drunk.

"How drunk are you?" I asked, instead of answering her.

"I was awesomely drunk until you walked into my apartment and killed my buzz in a horrible death," she retorted.

I eyed her for a second before I asked, "So, you're not drunk now?"

"No," she insisted. "But I wish to God I was because you're exhausting. Now, why in the hell would you want to go to dinner with me after all the horrible things I said to you?"

Well, I figured a person with her outspoken personality would appreciate honesty, so I honestly said, "Because every time I close my eyes, I relive last Friday when your tank-top did nothing to hide those perky tits of yours. I relive how your nipples were poking out and teasing me. I relive how, with every word you spewed at me, all I could do was imagine your mouth wrapped around my dick. I relive how weak my knees got when you turned to storm off, and I was graced with the view of that thick, luscious, drool-worthy ass and all the things that I want to do to it." That was about as honest as I could be with her, leaving out the stalking part of my obsession with her, of course.

Her chocolate eyes were blinking in a frantic manner, and I wondered if maybe she was having a stroke of some sort. After a few seconds, she finally found her voice. "You can't just come in here and tell a person those things," she announced.

This time, I put my hands on my hips as I peered down at her. "Why the hell not?" I waited for her to answer, but she didn't seem to have one. "Tell me you aren't attracted to me, and I'll leave, Lyrical," I said, realizing that I might be scaring the crap out of the poor ball of emotions.

Her eyes started darting all over the place, buying some time to come up with a lie of some sort-no doubt-but when she met my gaze again, she decided on honesty. "I can't," she whispered. "I can't, because I'm attracted to you."

Recalling what Rena had said earlier, my hand shot out, then I cradled the left side of her face, my fingers dancing in her hair, then asked the most important question of my life at the moment. "Do we really need to go to dinner first?"

Lyrical shook her head. "No," she said, her voice low and husky. "We don't need to go to dinner first."

Thank God.

CHAPTER 11

Lyrical ~
My conscience was screaming at me that we'd respect ourselves in the morning better if we really were drunk and could play this off as a stupid, reckless, drunken moment. It screamed at me to go take a few more shots, so that we'd have a legitimate reason behind the decision to be a hussy, but my body was yelling at me to do no such thing and go out and be the best hussy that we could be. My body wanted to experience everything that Nixon St. James was going to do to it stone-cold sober. Plus, when was I ever going to get the chance to experience someone that looked like Nixon?

Uh, never.

Then that thought brought me up short. I knew that I wasn't ugly by any stretch of the imagination, but I also knew that I wasn't in this man's league. Drunk or sober, it made no sense that he'd be attracted to me. My attraction to him was different; any woman with a pair of working eyes would find him sexy as hell. However, him attracted to me?

Nah, something was up.

Now, stop!

This was the part where you might let your insecurities reach up to start strangling you, but you don't want to go there; you wanted a clear head while you were in this game. If you started to analyze every flaw that you had versus every perfection that he had, then you'll start to cry, turning into an emotionally unstable lunatic, forcing him to call the police, and because your family never takes anything seriously, when the cops called them to verify your identity, they'd probably believe that this was some kind of elaborate hoax and *encourage* the cops to lock you up in the looney bin.

Well, no thanks.

No dick-*no matter how long my dry spell*-was worth ending up in a straitjacket, trying to prove my sanity. Besides, it was quite possible that the prosecution might have more witnesses to the contrary than the defense would have, trying to claim that I was sane; I wasn't exactly the friend-making type.

I shook my head, trying to dislodge all the craziness in my head, and focus on the issue at hand. "I think you need to leave," I said as sternly as I could.

His perfect hazel eyes blinked, and I could tell that he was surprised by the sudden change. "I thought-"

I waved away what he'd been about to say. "I know what you thought, but I'm coming to my senses," I informed him.

Nixon's brows shot upward. "And those senses are telling you to kick me out?"

My nose started to tingle, and I was instantly pissed that he was making me feel inadequate, though it was really just *me* making me feel that way. "It's telling me that this has to be some kind of joke," I snapped, feeling a bit foolish. "I stand by what I said earlier. There's no way someone who looks like you would be interested in someone who looks like me."

Nixon's face went from surprised to pissed. "Oh, really?"

I planted my hands on my hips, then leaned into the jackass. "Yeah, *really.*"

Then my brain short-circuited with what happened next; it was the only excuse that I had for what I let happen. Nixon's hands ran up my jaw until he had handfuls of my hair fisted in his grip, and then he slammed his lips down on mine.

Holy. Shit.

Not knowing what else to do, my hands went to his wrists, then I held on for dear life as Nixon St. James kissed the hell out of me. It was mere seconds before I opened for him, and the instant that his tongue swept in to play with mine, I knew that I was a goner.

The jerk could kiss.

He was kissing me the exact same way that every girl had ever wanted to be kissed; the same way that every female had ever fantasized when watching those horrible romantic comedies. Nixon was making me weak in the knees with the kiss that he was taking-*owning.*

It wasn't until my back hit the wall that I realized that he'd been walking us backwards, so that he could hold me captive against his tall, hard, muscular frame, and then I realized that I didn't mind it so much. In fact, I didn't mind it so much to the point that my hands traveled up the planes of his arms, biceps, and shoulders, then anchored around his neck. Unashamed, my hold on him was tighter than gripping knuckles on a rollercoaster, but I didn't care.

Nixon broke the kiss long enough to growl, "Do not tell me I shouldn't be attracted to you ever again, Lyrical." Me? I just whimpered. "I happen to think that you're sexy as fuck, and I've been thinking of nothing but fucking the holy living hell out of you for seven goddamn days."

Newsflash: Words were a powerful thing.

So, hearing this man tell me that he'd been doing nothing but thinking of fucking me for the past seven days? Well…there went Insecure Lyrical, and Let's-Be-A-Hussy Lyrical had taken her place. I grabbed onto Nixon St. James like he was a lifeboat, and we were on the Titanic.

My arms were like barnacles wrapped around the man, and I almost felt a little sorry for the poor bastard. I'd had one hell of a dry spell, and this poor, foolish, unsuspecting soul had no clue what he was in for. If I was going to get only one shot at this, then I was going to attack the man with no regrets. However, before I could figure out a way to attach myself to this man forever, Nixon pulled away, and I loved how labored his breathing was.

It meant that I wasn't the only desperate fool in the room.

His hands reached for the hem of my shirt when he said, "Why the fuck are you wearing clothes?"

I lifted my arms over my head to assist him. "I'll never wear them again," I offered.

My heart swelled and my hips twitched as I watched Nixon's hazel eyes darken when he got a look at my bra-cladded breast. His hands reached up to cup each one, and I made no effort to stop my moan.

"Why in the hell would you ever wear clothes in the first place just baffles my mind," he muttered.

I closed my eyes, then dropped my head back against the wall. His hands felt wonderful, even over the material of my bra. "Laws," I answered breathlessly. "It's against the law to walk around naked."

"Goddamn, laws," the man mumbled.

Then words escaped me when I felt him pull the cup of my bra down, then wrap his lips around my nipple. My mind was literally wrestling with letting him continue or dislodging him from my tit, so that I could drop to my knees. I was frantic in my desperation for pleasure, and let me tell you, it would please me greatly to weaken this man's knees. I wasn't a porn star by any means, but I was going to give this man my greatest efforts.

Ten years from now, when he was at the country club, reminiscing with his millionaire golfing buddies over great sex stories, I wanted him to include this night in his tales of crazy sex and debauchery. I wanted to debauch the hell out of this sexy man.

I opened my eyes, and the second that I looked down and saw nothing but sheer pleasure on his face as he suckled me, the fight was over. I reached down, then grabbing the hem of his shirt, I started pulling the fabric upwards, forcing him to detach himself from my breast. Luckily, Nixon didn't complain. Instead, he jumped onboard with my plan to get us naked, helping me pull his shirt up and over his head.

Holy. Fuck. Balls.

Nixon was fucking built like a goddamn Spartan warrior.

Like all stupid women, my mind instantly went to the six-pack abs that I *didn't* have, and suddenly, having my shirt off felt…jacked-up. While I did a good job of putting together camouflage outfits, once my pants came off, Nixon was going to get an eye full of a soft belly, thick thighs, and a jiggly ass, and that fucking sucked.

Jesus, why did I let him take my shirt off?

I should have left the shirt on to hide everything. Besides, all he needed was access to my nether regions, right? He didn't need to actually *see* them. Insecure Lyrical was steadily making an appearance again, and Let's-Be-A-Hussy Lyrical was quickly giving up the fight.

"Nixon, hold on," I urged, pushing at his chest; his smooth, muscled, rock-hard chest.

Nixon blinked down at me in confusion. "What? Why?"

My brown eyes met his hazel ones, and I didn't mean to turn into a spaz and ruin the passion, but I did. "Can...can I put my shirt back on?"

It took a moment, but the second that it dawned on him what I was asking and why, Nixon's features softened, and while I hadn't expected the words that came out of his mouth, if it was possible to fall in love in an instant, that instant would be this one.

He leaned in to kiss the corner of my mouth. "Why don't we *both* put our shirts back on?" he suggested.

"I'll understand if you want to leave," I muttered, knowing that I ruined the moment.

"Oh, make no mistake, baby," he smirked. "We're still fucking."

Well...okay, then.

CHAPTER 12

Nixon ~
It was probably super insensitive of me, but I knew that I couldn't fix her self-esteem issues tonight, so I was willing to compromise and do whatever it took to make her comfortable enough to let me fuck her; I would work on her self-confidence tomorrow.

Then the next day.

Then the day after that if I needed to.

Then for the rest of our lives if she wasn't magically cured of her insecurities by the day after next.

Her eyes were full of so many emotions that she looked sweet and endearing. "You still want to do this?"

I reached down, grabbed both of our shirts, then quickly threw mine back on. When I started pulling her shirt back down over her head, I said, "Hell, yeah, I still want to do this."

"But...but I just spazzed out on you," she informed me as if I hadn't been here to witness it. "Why aren't you running away like any sane man would?"

Tugging on the hem of her shirt to make sure that she was covered again, I looked into her eyes, then said, "Because your sexy outweighs your crazy?" I voiced it like a question, and the girl didn't disappoint.

Her little hands started flailing at my chest like a flapping bird. "Get out," she snapped. "Get the hell out of my house, you jerk."

Instead of conceding to her wishes, I grabbed both of her wild hands with one hand, then wrapped my other hand around her waist, turning her until I had her pushed up against the wall. I had her caged in with her cheek pressed against the wall, my body covering her entire back.

My right hand had a death grip on her hands-*because, well...she was crazy*-but my left hand was already snaking its way down her stomach, over her pelvis, and it didn't stop until it was nestled in between her thighs.

Now, while most guys would do almost anything to get laid, I wasn't most guys. Of course, don't get me wrong; nothing on this earth felt better than sinking your dick into a warm, wet, willing pussy, but I didn't lose my mind if it's been longer than a month.

So, I wasn't manhandling Lyrical because I needed to get laid, or now that I'd had her tit in my mouth, I felt like she owed it to me to follow through. No. I was manhandling this nutjob because she'd been so spectacularly vulnerable when she'd asked if she could put her shirt back on that I couldn't think of anything else but trying to make this woman see herself through my eyes. For the most part, I was an asshole and not very people-friendly, but something about Lyrical called to the part of me that wasn't a complete dick. The part that I reserved for my friends and family wanted to get to know Lyrical.

I started rubbing her center through the fabric of her simple cotton pants, and I could feel the heat from her pussy warming my fingers. Now, while I did imply that I wouldn't cut my arm off for some sex, having my hand between Lyrical's thighs, feeling the heat coming off her, had me damn near in a frenzy.

Lyrical immediately stopped struggling when I started rubbing her pussy, and she let out the sweetest, softest, sexiest moan. "Oh, God…"

"Here's the thing, Lyrical," I said, my voice a whisper next to her ear. "I don't care if you are crazy. I don't care about anything other than getting inside that sweet, hot, tight pussy of yours." She rubbed her ass against my groin, and I took that as a positive sign. "And if we have to be damn near fully clothed to make that happen, then that's what we're going to do."

"Nixon…"

I didn't give her a chance to argue with me-*which, let's face it, odds were that she was going to*-before I was releasing her crazy hands, then unbuttoning her pants, pulling down her zipper next. My right hand was inside her panties within milliseconds, and my fingers were already parting her slick folds, tunneling their way inside her pussy.

"Christ, you're so fucking wet," I rasped against her neck, and she really was.

Lyrical was so wet that I could hear the slickness that my fingers were playing in over the sounds of our heavy breathing. Still, even though she was wet as fuck, she'd already tried to kick me out twice, so I needed her *out of her mind* with lust. I needed to make sure that she was so lust-drunk that she wouldn't think about kicking me out until the morning.

I wanted to worship this woman all night. Really, I wanted to. I wanted to take my time kissing every inch of her body and tasting every secret that she had, but I knew that I was working against the insanity that resided inside that pretty little head of hers. So, while I used my right hand to distract her crazy, I used my left hand to unbutton, then unzip my jeans.

Have you ever tried to undress yourself with one hand while controlling a crazy person with the other? The shit wasn't fun.

Or easy.

When I finally managed to get my jeans down to my thighs, I pulled my fingers out of her cunt, then used both my hands to push her pants down over her magnificent ass. I hated how this was rushed and sloppy, but the little whimper that had escaped when I had removed my fingers from her pussy told me that she was onboard with this, and we'd work on finesse and grace later.

I grabbed onto Lyrical's hips, angled her back, then grabbing my dick in one hand, I lined it up against her soaked pussy, finally slamming home. I couldn't stop my eyes from rolling to the back of my head at how incredible she felt wrapped around me. I knew that she wasn't a virgin, but it'd had to be years since she'd been fucked because she was tighter than anything that I'd ever experienced. Lyrical was hot, tight, and perfect.

Her hands slapped against the wall as her back arched at my invasion. "Nixon…"

I completely ignored her cries, and with my hands on her hips, I stared down and watched as her ass bounced and rippled with each push into her hot, tight, perfect body. "Jesus Christ."

Not worrying that I was taking The Lord's name in vain, Lyrical immediately started pushing back with each thrust, actively fucking me back. "Oh, God…" she moaned. "Harder, Nixon…fuck me harder."

Not a problem.

My hands tightened on her hips, then I rammed my cock into this girl like it was the last time that I was ever going to get pussy. I drilled my dick inside her so hard and so deep that I was certain that she was going to be sore in the morning. At least, I hoped that she would be. I wanted to leave a lasting impression on this woman, so that I'd be invited back here.

"Is that hard enough, baby," I grunted in her ear. "Or do you need it harder?" Now, while I was giving it to her hard enough to leave bruises, if she wanted it harder, then I was going to do everything in my power to damage the both of us.

"Oh, Christ…that's perfect…" she cried out. "I think…I think I'm already going to cum…oh, God…Nixon…"

Praise Jesus and Halle-fucking-lujiah.

Still, because I wasn't so egotistical that I thought that I was a god in bed or anything, I figured that Lyrical's quick and early eagerness, partnered with how tight her pussy was, was a clear indication that it'd been ages since this girl had been fucked good, long, and hard.

So, I was about to give her my best dirty talk when she went and detonated all over me. Lyrical came hard around my dick, and it almost made me explode prematurely inside her. Luckily, my male ego was holding on for dear life with the determination that we were going to give Lyrical at least one more orgasm before we gave up the fight.

Seriously, men's egos were so fucking ridiculous.

Nonetheless, I rode her through her orgasm, not letting up one bit as her pussy contracted, strangling the fuck out of my dick.

"Nixon, I..." she trailed off, letting out a small moan, making me feel like a king. "I...stop, please...I can't..."

Stop?

Not on her fucking life.

Now, if she'd meant it, that'd be one thing, but she didn't mean it, and how did I know this you ask? I knew it because her lips were telling me one thing, but the fact that her ass was pushing back against me, begging for more, told me her truth.

"No," I hissed, pushing into her harder. "Give me one more, and then I'll stop." I tightened my hands on her hips, then pounded into her deeper than I thought that I ever could. "Come on, Lyrical. Give me one more, baby."

"Oh, God..." she moaned as I felt her body tightening up again.

"That's it," I coaxed. "Be a good girl for me and cum all over my cock again, so that I can finally fill you up, Lyrical."

My words must have worked, because the next thing that I knew, Lyrical was convulsing all over my cock as she screamed my name. *"Nixon..."*

Fuck.

Yeah.

Less than five pumps later, I was cumming inside her tight, soaked, spasming heat. *"Motherfucker,"* I hissed, and nothing had ever felt so good, but then it occurred to me that nothing in my life had ever felt so good because I'd never had sex without a condom.

At least, not before now.

CHAPTER 13

Lyrical ~
"So, then he just left?" Rena asked, bewildered and confused.
"Well, to be fair, he left in the morning, Rena," Alice said, coming to Nixon's defense. "It's not like he made a run for it while she was still dripping on the floor."
I winced.
"Gee, Alice. Thanks for that visual," I grimaced.
She laughed as she was sprawled out across my bed, not caring if she was wrinkling her outfit. "Well, it's true," she defended.
We were at my apartment, getting ready for our monthly girls' night out, and Alice and I were already finished getting ready. We were just waiting on Rena to finish taming her blonde locks, something that she liked to complain about. I was sitting on the dowry trunk at the foot of my bed while Rena was doing her hair in front of my vanity.
Looking in the mirror, Rena said, "I just don't understand. You guys screwed all night long, then in the morning, he just…left. With no talk about seeing you later or calling you or anything?"
I let out a sigh.
After Nixon had pounded me up against the wall, he had redressed us, and then walked us to my bedroom where he'd done the most amazing, caring, silly, wonderful thing that anyone had ever done for me. This perfection of a man had pulled the covers back on the bed, pushed me onto the mattress, walked over to the light switch, turned it off, got undressed in the dark, then had crawled into bed with me where he had undressed me, letting me hide underneath the protection of the covers.
From there, he had spent all night just straight fucking me. Not once had Nixon tried to explore my body or push me out of my comfort zone. He had kept his lips limited to my lips, my face, and my neck. His hands had stayed planted on the mattress, on my hips, or around my neck the entire time.

Nixon hadn't tried to touch or kiss the rest of my body, not even once.

Nixon had also only taken me missionary, from behind doggy-style, and from behind in spoon fashion, but mostly missionary. He hadn't asked me to get on top or take over, and he'd done his best to make it an enjoyable experience while catering to my insecurities. Unfortunately, in the light of morning, I'd woken up feeling idiotically foolish, especially since I'd never had problems with sex before.

Sure, Nixon had been the first man to blow my mind with his talents in the bedroom, but I'd never been afraid of sex to the point where a man had ever *had* to screw me in the dark. Something had misfired in my brain when I'd gotten a good look at how hard and fit his body was, and while I hadn't touched his dick at all last night, his apparent size had been super noticeable when he had slammed into me against the wall.

"Well, he did leave," I reiterated.

"Wow," Rena replied, surprised. "I hadn't taken him for being an outright jerk."

I could feel the bed's movements behind me. "What are you not telling us, Lyric?" my sister asked.

Now, stop!

This was the part where you would love to tell people that shit's none of their business, but you don't. There was a reason that Rena was my best friend, and that I got along so well with my sister. See, they were crazy, too.

So, if I told them to mind their own business, then that was a surefire way to start a fight where the cops would be called, then we'd all be arrested. Then, since my parents couldn't afford to bail both their daughters out of jail, they'd bail Alice out, leaving me to rot for what should just be a mutual combat call, but will no doubt be an assault charge because Alice didn't look like the type to start a fight with anyone, but let me tell youuuuuuuuuuuuuu…

Not to mention, Rena would most likely break out of her handcuffs, escape the law, and then become a fugitive for life, and none of us wanted that; Rena was irreplaceable.

"Ugh," I huffed-rather dramatically, I might add. "Fine. I might have woken up first, left a note next to his pillow, telling him that I had a swell time, but I forgot I had to go to Minneapolis for the weekend and to please lock the door on his way out."

"Why Minneapolis?" Alice asked, clearly losing focus of her original question.

"Why not Minneapolis?" I countered.

Rena stopped whatever she'd been doing, then turned, eyeing me. "So, that's why you were knocking on my door at all hours of the morning?"

"Maybe," I mumbled.

"Oh, my God!" she screeched, rightfully so. "You said you were feeling like crud and needed some love." She wasn't lying, I had said that. "I took you in, cared for you, and worried about you. I nursed you back to health, damn it."

Alice threw up a finger. "Uh, did you really?" she questioned. "I mean, if she wasn't sick in the first place, then you really kind of didn't nurse her back to health. She was already healthy."

Rena slapped her hands on her hips, forgetting about her hair. Her blue peepers widened really quickly as she said, "I'm leaving the damn thing down. I don't have time for this. And, yes, Alice. It does count. Her being a lying liar does not negate my healing efforts."

Alice cocked her head. "You got a point," she conceded before turning back to me. "So, then you hid out at Rena's until Nixon left?"

"Something like that," I mumbled.

"No," Rena corrected. "Exactly like that."

"He didn't leave a number or anything?" Alice asked as she stood up to give herself one final look in the full-length mirror, even though she didn't need to. She looked perfect in her black top, pale pink flare skirt, and black heels. The outfit showed off her slim figure and killer legs.

Rena was dressed in a men's blue button-up shirt, a pair of hip-hugger jeans, and a pair of matching blue sandals. Rena liked to dance, so she wasn't a fan of heels unless shit was formal. Still, no matter, with Rena's figure, it didn't matter what she wore: she was always a knockout.

I was probably the least dressed up. I'd thrown on a green tank-top, a pair of black hip-huggers, and had finished the look off with a pair of black heels, and they were taller than Alice's because I was the shortest of our group. Now, while Alice's hair was braided into a loose French braid, and Rena's was flowing down her back, I'd thrown my brown tresses up in a messy bun. Any more effort than that, then I would have voted to stay home and get drunk.

"I didn't see a note of any kind," I answered Alice.

Rena rolled her eyes.

Rude.

"Maybe because a man like Nixon St. James has, oh, I don't know, maybe a smidge of pride in his backbone and knew a brushoff when he saw one?"

I gasped. "Hey! There's no way he could possibly know that I didn't really have a trip scheduled to Minneapolis."

Rena cocked her head to the side. "We have internet-stalked these men enough to know that he comes from a family that boasts his father as a judge, his mother as a lawyer, his brother as a doctor, and his other brother as a lawyer," she recited. "I'm going to go out on a limb and say that the real estate mogul probably has one working brain cell, if not two." She threw her arms up as she injected some real enthusiasm into her next words. "Of course, he knew you ditched him, Lyric."

I finally stood up, knowing that we were getting ready to head out to the bar. "I don't think so," I argued.

"Well," Alice said, chiming in, "I think I'm going to have to agree with

Rena on this one, Lyric. I mean, did you mention how you needed some sleep for your upcoming trip at all? Did you even pretend to pack or anything?"

"Of course, I didn't mention my trip. It was a *forgotten* trip," I reminded her. "Besides, we didn't spend…uh, a whole lot of time talking last night."

"Okay. I'm just going to say it," Alice announced, gearing up for something big. "We've all been avoiding the elephant in the room, and I say no more."

I looked between her and Rena. "What elephant?"

There was no elephant.

There'd never been an elephant.

My shame and embarrassment were usually all out in the open for everyone to enjoy.

"How big is his dick?" Alice asked.

"Is he good in the sack?" Rena asked at the same time, overlapping Alice's question.

My eyes widened. Did these women have no shame? No sense of respect or privacy? "I am not going to ans-*owwww!*"

Alice had me by my ear. "Don't make me waterboard you, Lyric," she threatened. "I will so torture the hell out of you."

"Oh, my God," I yelped. "Rena? Are you just going to let her t-"

"Hell yeah, I am," Rena replied, interrupting my pleas for help. "Answer the questions."

"Jesus. Fine. Fine," I cried, surrendering like a pussy. "Let go of my goddamn ear, Alice."

Alice let go of my ear, then both women stood in front of me with their arms crossed over their chests, waiting for me to give up the goods. "Well?" Rena prompted.

I took a deep breath, then huffed it out dramatically, letting them know that I was clearly against this sort of interrogation. However, my theatrics didn't faze either wench. *"Fiiiiiiiiiine,"* I drawled out. "I'm not sure the size because I didn't have a ruler on me, but he was big enough to bottom out a few times. As for his Yelp sex review, a solid ten stars out of five."

Really, he deserved a twenty-star rating.

CHAPTER 14

Nixon ~
I sat on the barstool, drinking my beer, as I waited for my jackass brothers to stop laughing.
Fucking assholes.
"Oh, this is priceless," Lincoln said through his unappreciated laughter. "She actually snuck out of her *own* home, pretending she was leaving for Minneapolis. Jesus Christ, Nix, how bad in the sack are you?"
I flipped him off. After all, that question didn't warrant an actual answer. I didn't suck in the sack, goddamn it. Still, I didn't want to explain to Linc and Jackson that Lyrical was crazy. I wanted them to meet her first, then grow to love her before I explained that she was a bit off in her pretty head.
Now, while Jackson wasn't being as big of a dick as Lincoln was, he was close. "I don't think that even during my worst performance, I've ever had a woman sneak out of her *own* home just to avoid me."
It hadn't been my proudest moment.
Now, normally, I wouldn't share such personal details with others, but these were my brothers, so they didn't count as others. Plus, I needed to talk to someone about this madness because, much like Jackson, I'd never had a woman willingly flee the comforts of her own home just to get away from me. Maybe I needed to confess to them that Lyrical was actually a little touched in the head.
"It wasn't the sex," I insisted. "Not to...uh, brag or...tell her business, but...she responded eagerly to everything I did to her."
Truthfully, I hadn't even done all that much to her. Knowing that she was neurotic about her body image, I'd done my best to curb most of my wants and a lot of my needs. Because let me tell you, I had *needed* to eat her pussy. I had *needed* to suck on her tits. I had *needed* to choke her with my cock. I had *needed* to consume every physical inch of her perfect body.
It'd been hard to limit myself to only fucking her in certain positions and

not touching her everywhere that I could. However, Lyrical had accused me of not paying attention when she had spazzed out, and that hadn't been true; I'd been paying nothing but attention to her.

Now, while not being an expert on women and their neuroses, I'd done my best to calm her fears but still reap the rewards. The small glimpse that I'd seen of her when she'd had her shirt off had been enough to know that she would look fantastic naked. Her tits were a perfect handful, and she was soft like a woman was supposed to be. I just wished that I could have convinced her of that last night.

Lincoln took a drink of his beer before saying, "Maybe she just wanted to get laid and didn't want an awkward morning-after."

"Or could be that she thought *you* just wanted to get laid, and so she was giving you an out, Nix," Jackson suggested.

I didn't remark on either possibility, instead I signaled the bartender for another round.

Huxley's was a low-key bar where you went if you wanted to just enjoy a beer and bullshit. They had a jukebox and brought in a DJ during the late hours, but for the most part, it was perfect for uneventful relaxing. It was why I had suggested that we come here instead of a club. I wasn't in the mood to party or fight the crowds for much-needed drinks. Lyrical really fucked me up with her disappearing act this morning, and so I needed some quality time with my brothers, even if they were both idiots.

I turned back to face my brothers just as Linc asked, "What are you going to tell Mom and Dad? I mean, I can't see them taking this news well, Nix."

Jackson's head nodded in affirmation. "Yeah. They're really looking forward to the wedding and the baby."

I was sitting in between my brothers at the bar, so it was hard to stink-eye them both at the same time. So, I picked Lincoln first because he usually deserved it more than Jackson did. "Somehow, I doubt Lyrical would be open to marriage right now. Never mind a baby."

"Good thing you made sure to wrap it up last night then," Jackson smirked. "Seeing as how you're so responsible and all." When I turned, I tried to poker face him, but my wince came across loud and clear, then I felt Jackson's hand slap across the back of my head at my obvious body language. "Do not even tell me you didn't use protection, Nix," he growled.

Awe, fuck.

There were times when Jackson being a doctor sucked.

"Jacks-"

He started shaking his head at me. "No, Nixon," he said, interrupting my ready excuse. "I see what happens to kids that are not wanted. Keep having unprotected sex, and I will cut your baby maker off with my scalpel."

I rubbed the back of my head. "Hey!"

"What?" he bit out.

I leaned into my eldest brother. "Don't lump me in with the losers that you come across, Jackson," I huffed. "If I got Lyrical knocked up, I'd do the right thing."

"Doing the right thing is not the same as *wanting* the child," he countered.

I tried not to take his words personally because I knew how my brother felt about children and their neglect. "I'd want any child I made, Jackson," I said more calmly. "You know this."

"I know, Nix," he replied, sighing heavily. "It's just...I'd hate for the mother of my niece or nephew to run off with the kid that we'll never see again, and all because you sucked in bed." Linc laughed, and just like that, they were both back to being assholes.

"I don't suck in bed, you fucks," I mumbled.

"And still, a woman that doesn't know you well enough to know you're a complete dick fled the confines of her own home just to ditch you," Linc recited. "Sounds like you suck in bed to me, Nix."

I flipped Lincoln off again. "I'll have you two fuckwads know that Lyrical fled because she was so overcome with emotions of our night together that she didn't know how to process them all," I retorted. "She just panicked. That's all."

"Yeah, disappointment, dissatisfaction, and sorrow are some pretty serious emotions," Jackson chuckled, and then I flipped *him* off.

I swiveled around in my barstool until I was facing the crowd. It wasn't super packed, but there were enough people to make it interesting. A few couples, but mostly groups of friends or co-workers drinking the day away. I scanned the faces of the groups of women that weren't accompanied by men, and I imagined that they were all pretty sane. Too bad that wasn't doing it for me anymore. No. I was knowingly obsessing over a little ball of insanity and probably homicidal intent, and as I looked over at my brother, I'd always thought that it'd be Lincoln who would end up with a crazy wife. I mean, seriously.

"Look, why don't you just stop by her house when she gets back from her imaginary trip to Minneapolis, and ask her what's the deal?" Jackson suggested.

I turned to him, narrowing my eyes at his maturity and sensible rationale. "That's a horrible idea," I scoffed, though it really wasn't. However, I wasn't about to tell him that I was half-ass chicken shit of the truth, whatever it was.

Before Jackson could call me an idiot, Lincoln let out a low whistle, and then turned towards us, and he was laughing like a goddamn loon. Mom and Dad really should have given me sisters, instead of these two buffoons.

"What?" Jackson asked.

Lincoln had that smile on his face. You know, the one where he was about to commit some sort of atrocity against nature, and all that we could do was stand by and watch because no one's figured out how to rein in Lincoln's warped mind? Yeah, *that* smile.

"I guess your girl wrapped up shit in Minneapolis faster than she anticipated," he smirked, then jerked his head towards the front door where three women had just walked in. The first being Rena, the second being a slim, pretty, auburn-haired beauty, and the last being the crazy woman that was supposed to be in Minneapolis.

"Motherfucker," I hissed.

"Hold up, wait," Jackson sputtered. "Are you telling me one of those women is Lyrical?"

"The brunette," Linc so helpfully provided.

"Holy shit," he whistled out. "Look at that ass. I-"

"Don't even finish that sentence, Jackson," I growled, turning towards my eldest brother, ready to slap his face with my invisible glove to make an appointment for pistols at dawn.

He threw up his hands in surrender, making sure not to spill his beer. "Oh, hey. Calm down, little brother," he laughed. "Her ass is all yours."

Then Lincoln really started laughing when he said, "Holy shit, Nixon. You fucked her all night long last night, but she's out tonight with her girls? Dude, you must really suck in bed."

"She bailed on you because she didn't have the heart to tell you, I bet," Jackson added.

"Fuck you, both," I growled. "Just. Fuck. You. Both."

This was not good.

I could feel insecurity and that green-eyed little monster making their appearance, and Lyrical really should have stayed her ass on her imaginary trip to Minneapolis.

CHAPTER 15

Lyrical ~
We'd made it to Huxley's fairly early, so we'd been able to find a booth immediately. As soon as my ass hit the bench, Alice piped up. "I'll go order the first round." With that announcement, she flounced-*yes, flounced*-over to the bar to get the first round.

"So, what's on the agenda tonight," Rena asked.

"I thought we were just coming out to have a couple of drinks and gossip," I replied.

Rena rolled her eyes. "Says the girl who got her world rocked last night," she retorted. "Do you have any idea how long it's been since I've been laid?"

Since Rena was my best friend, I knew that answer. "Stewart, the guy you met at High Café seven months ago," I announced.

"Yeah," she confirmed. "Stewart, *seven* months ago, and he sucked."

"Oh, hey," I said comfortingly. "You did say he did give it his all, though. The poor man did try to please you and your impossible demands."

Rena's blue eyes widened. "My impossible demands?" She snorted her disbelief. "I wasn't even asking for an orgasm, Lyric. I was just hoping that he'd last longer than five minutes each round. It was horrible."

"So, we're here to get laid?" I asked because I needed absolute clarification on my role here tonight.

Alice placed the bucket of beers in the middle of the table, plopped her ass down next to Rena, then asked, "We're trolling for penis tonight?"

I plucked a beer out of the bucket. "*I'm* not, but apparently Rena is," I clarified.

Alice nodded in thought, and as she grabbed her own beer, she said, "Well, good. That makes sense, and it's actually a good thing."

Rena glanced over at her. "It is? Why?"

Alice took a very big, very construction-worker-gulp of her beer before saying, "Because while I was waiting for Mr. Bartender to fill the bucket full of beers, I happened to give the room a curious glance, and I notice three very hot, very built, very drool-worthy men sitting at the bar together, and-"

"Probably married or gay," Rena huffed, interrupting Alice.

Alice ignored her. *"Annnnnnnnnnd,* due to my diligent internet-stalking, I was able to identify those three male specimens of perfection as the St. James brothers."

Rena started choking on her drink, and I turned into a statue, hoping that my complete stillness would turn me invisible somehow. Hey, don't judge. It could work.

After Rena got herself under control, she shot Alice an incredulous look. "Are you sure?"

"Don't look and be all high-school-girl obvious, but I am absolutely sure," she said, the biggest smile on her face.

Oh, no...I knew that smile.

"Hey, Rena, you want to follow me to the jukebox?"

"Don't you dar-"

"Absolutely," Rena said, already laughing with anticipation of whatever Alice had planned.

Alice reached over, then patted my arm. "You'll thank us for this one day, Lyric," she said as she stood up. "If not, well, remember how much you love me, and that I'm your only sibling."

Everything in me wanted to scan the faces at the bar, but I was supposed to be in Minneapolis, so I had to act like I didn't know that Nixon was here. With his brothers, no less.

So, instead of acting like a bigger spaz than I'd already had, I grabbed my phone, then pretended to answer a text as I sipped my beer, all calm, cool, collected, and sophisticated like. However, let me assure you-*in case you were confused*-that I was *not* feeling calm, cool, collected, or sophisticated. However, to be fair, I'd never been sophisticated, so that was a rather lofty goal to try to accomplish in the first place.

Alice and Rena made it back at the same exact second a beat boomed out of the jukebox, and immediately recognizing the song, I glared at the two people that I hated most in the world right now. "You did not just-"

I stopped when I realized that they'd had. Eddie Money's Take Me Home Tonight started thumping around the room, and I just knew that this was going to be something worthy of its own YouTube clip, and that we were going to be the stars.

Goddamn it.

Suddenly-but not surprisingly-Rena started singing into her beer bottle, and she was looking right at me, so that the entire bar knew that I was being serenaded. "'I can feel you breathe. I can feel your heart beat faster'," she crooned, and then Alice-the traitor-joined in for the chorus. "'Take me home tonight. I don't want to let you go till you see the light. Take me home tonight. Listen, honey. Just like Ronnie sang…'"

I turned-*mortified in case that wasn't clear*-to face my sister as she belted out Ronnie Spector's part. "'Be my little baby...'"

Then, just when you thought that it couldn't get any worse, I started hearing whoops and hollers from the spectators in the room. They were encouraging these two psychos, not realizing the havoc that they were encouraging that was about to be released. They had no idea of the evils that these two were capable of, and here they were, just egging them on in this madness.

I watched-again, mortified-as Rena and Alice got up from the booth, and then started prancing around the room, singing at me from all different directions. These fools were singing a song about asking someone to take them home in front of several single men, and I just hoped that they were prepared for when those single men started approaching our table, thinking that this performance was our ritual mating call.

Then things got worse.

Oh, how could things get any worse you ask?

Now, stop!

The climax of the song started, and Alice and Rena, in a very concert-at-Madison-Square-Garden fashion, stopped in front of our booth, then handed the lip syncing over to me. I had a split second to decide if I was going to ruin their fun and the entertainment of the rest of the bar, or if I was going to join in the madness and give everyone a good laugh.

I wanted *so badly* to ruin everyone's good time because I did *not* relish becoming a YouTube clip. Still, I looked into the faces of my sister and best friend, and I couldn't do it. These were the best people that I knew, and no matter how insane they were, I knew that they only had my best interests at heart. If we ever ended up in jail, it would be because whatever had gotten us there had started out in good faith; I was sure of it.

So, in true rock star fashion, I pointed at the two lunatics, then channeled my inner rock star. I waited for the music to drop, then away I went. "'Take me home tonight. I don't want to let you go till you see the light...'"

"'Oh, oh, oh, oh, ohhhhh...'" Alice jumped in while Rena joined me in the second hook.

We lip synced the shit out of the rest of the song, and we got a chorus of laughs, applause, and cattle calls once the song faded away. Feeling the energy, I couldn't help it. I laughed along with them in our booth like idiotic teenagers, feeling good. It was silly, ridiculous, and utterly embarrassing, but fun. Granted, fun usually *was* silly, ridiculous, and embarrassing.

"Oh, God," I laughed. "I can't believe we did that."

"Oh, hey, look," Rena chuckled. "If you weren't going to balls up and go drag Nixon into the bathroom to blow him, then we had to come up with a way to give him the hint that you were down with round two."

My eyes rounded. "And *that* was your best idea?"

Alice laughed. "No," she answered. "We had way better ones, but none as fun as that."

"Newsflash, you twits," I snorted, "I don't find humiliation fun at all."

"How was that humiliating?" Rena asked, right after finishing up her beer.

"Oh, c'mon," I groaned. "You know there's at least one person who recorded that and is going to post it all over the internet."

"Yeah, but-"

"Hello, ladies," came a smooth, deep, rich voice, effectively cutting off the debate about our future internet sensationalism.

All three of our heads turned to look up into the face of a very nice-looking man with blonde hair, blue eyes, and a sexy, smirky smile.

Not bad.

Luckily for him, Rena was looking to get her bell rung, and I was pretty sure that Alice was on board with some naked time, too. As a matter of fact, I was pretty sure that Alice was long overdue more so than Rena was.

"Well, hello there," Alice purred, confirming my suspicions.

He glanced back at his table really quickly, then said, "We were wondering why that song?"

Why that song, indeed.

CHAPTER 16

Nixon ~

I saw that asshole approached their table, and as I glanced over at his friends, I noticed how their numbers lined up, three girls for three guys.

Yeah, this shit was not happening.

When the girls had started singing, I couldn't help but laugh and enjoy their spectacle along with everyone else. It'd been cute, fun, and unexpected, and their song choice had been all the hint that I'd needed. Though I didn't know who the third girl was, I already knew that Rena was on my side, so there was a strong possibility that she had played that song for me and Lyrical. Now, if she hadn't...well, it didn't matter. I'd already convinced myself that she had, so that means she did.

"Looks like she forgot all about you while she was in Minneapolis, Nix," Linc remarked as he took in the guy that had approached their table.

My insides hollowing out was not a pleasant feeling. "He could be approaching Rena or the other girl," I pointed out.

"Which one is Rena," Jackson asked.

"The blonde," I answered automatically. "I'm not sure who the other woman is, but it was those two that had started the show, so maybe it's one of them who caught his eye."

Linc snorted. "Yeah, Nix. His eye and the eye of the other two dudes he's with. Do the math, little brother."

I took my eyes off Lyrical's table long enough to glare at Lincoln. "I did, fuckface. That's why you and Jackson are going to go over there with me, so that there's no room for confusion as to who belongs to whom."

Jackson choked on his beer as Linc said, "Uh...I'm pretty sure we can't just go over there and claim them like that, Nix."

"Why not?"

Linc's face took on a bewildered look. "Uh, because this is America, and you can't just own another human being. It's sort of against the law."

"I beg to differ." Did I mention Jackson as being an asshole earlier? Because if I did, I take it back now as he refuted Lincoln's claim. "You can legally own another human being under the ceremony of marriage, dear brother."

"Are you for real right now?" Linc asked, still bewildered. "That's a partnership, Jackson. You don't suddenly *own* another person just because you say 'I do'. It doesn't work that way."

Jackson snorted. "The fuck you don't," he countered. "The woman who becomes my wife is going to be owned and operated by me, and only me." He smirked Linc's way. "But, hey, if your wife is going to be free to do whatever she wants, then more power to you, Lincoln. I just know that I couldn't do it."

Lincoln arched a brow coolly. "My wife will do whatever I tell her," he stated with an authority that he knew he didn't possess.

"Not if she's free and can't be owned," Jackson laughed.

"Fuck you, Jacks-"

"Dudes! Can we focus here on the asshole currently trying to lure Lyrical home, instead of the fictitious wives that you guys don't even have yet?" I snapped, seriously losing it. I mean, I literally spent all night inside Lyrical, so there was no reason that she should be talking to another guy right now.

No. Reason. At. All.

"Damn, Nix," Lincoln whistled. "Never seen you lose your shit over a woman before."

"I am not losing my shit," I lied through my clenched teeth. "Now, here's what's going to happen. We're all going over there-I don't care which female you guys claim-but know that you're claiming one, and we are going to sit with them, drink with them, maybe dance, and just have a merry fucking good time for the rest of the night. Got it?"

I didn't wait for them to answer. I slammed my empty beer bottle down on the bar, hopped off the barstool, then stomped my way over to Lyrical and her friends like a spoiled child having the worst tantrum in history. However, before anyone judges, the tantrum was warranted, because with every second that passed where Lyrical was actually chatting it up with another man, well…it gave credit to Lincoln and Jackson's opinions that I sucked in bed, and *I did not fucking suck in bed.*

I also knew that my brothers were right behind me. That was one of the great things about my family; we always had each other's backs, even if we were wrong. We'd work to get each other right after the fact, but we still went all out for one another.

I completely ignored Lyrical's astounded expression as I saddled up next to Blondie. I approached the table like I had every right, and as far as I was concerned, I did. After last night and her phantom Minneapolis trip this morning…well, I absolutely *did* have the right to harass her in public.

"Hey, baby," I said, greeting her as if we were actually dating. "I take it you didn't see us sitting at the bar?"

Mr. Surfer-Me-Blonde glanced at me, then looked ready to say something, but before he could utter something that was going to get him popped in the face, Lincoln dropped down to sit next to Rena, then placed his arm around her.

"You didn't get my text that we were at the bar?" he asked her, and I really did have great brothers when they weren't being assholes.

Lyrical looked like she was in the middle of a stroke as she scooted out of the booth, then came to stand next to me. "Nixon-"

Jackson took that opportunity to take her place in the booth. He placed his arms on the table, then leaned into the third girl as if he'd been dating her for years. "Hey, baby," he cooed. "Climb over the table and come sit next to me. I've missed you."

"Oh, hey," Blondie said, taking a step back from the table. "Sorry. I didn't realize-"

Ignoring whatever Lyrical had been about to say, I turned, then gave the unwelcomed guy my undivided attention. "Oh, yeah," I said, trying to sound as casual as possible. "A little miscommunication, but these ladies are with us."

Luckily for him, he took it all in stride as he gave everyone a big smile. "My mistake. It was nice meeting you ladies, nevertheless," he replied before turning around, then heading back to his table.

The second that he was out of earshot, Lyrical hissed, "What in the hell was that all about?"

I grabbed her by her arm, then shoved her back into the booth, caging her in between Jackson and me. I twisted in my seat to face her. "How was Minneapolis?"

She had enough shame to look uncomfortable, but she didn't back down from her lie. "Uh, great," she mumbled. "Got a lot done."

I wanted to throttle her.

Straight up strangle her in front of everyone in here.

Still, no matter how strong the urge, I knew that there was no way that Lincoln would be able to get me off with so many witnesses. I was going to have to strangle her later when we were in private.

"So, let's table your trip to Minneapolis for now. Introduce me to your friends instead," I said in lieu of manslaughter.

It took her exactly five seconds to decide what to do, but I could see the fight go out of her right before she made the introductions. "Nixon, you already know Rena..."

"Hey, Nixon," Rena said, her face a full-watt smile.

"Nice to see you again, Rena," I greeted back.

Then Lyrical jerked her head towards the other woman. "That's my sister, Alice. Alice meet Nixon St. James. He's the guy who owns the building I live in."

Ouch.

I was the guy that owned the building where she lived?

I mean, I was…but fuck…

"Hi, Nixon," she replied. "It's nice to meet you."

"Likewise," I said, doing my best to inject some genuine interest, but I was more concerned with Lyrical than making new friends. "These are my brothers, Lincoln and Jackson. Lincoln and Jackson, Alice and Rena." After that shit effort, I turned back to face Lyrical. "Get your shit and let's go."

Her face took on the perfect amount of outrage. "What? You can't just deman-"

"If you don't want an audience for a huge ass fight over your fake trip to Minneapolis, then I suggest you get your shit and *let's go,* Lyrical," I snapped, and I wasn't kidding.

"You better go, Lyrical," Jackson suggested. "He's a jerk on the best of days, but when he's pissed, he's an outright asshole."

Lyrical turned her outrage towards Jackson. "He is not an asshole," she exclaimed, defending me, and that's when I knew that it was love.

CHAPTER 17

Lyrical ~
The ride to Nixon's place was quiet and filled with tension, but it was my fault; I owned it. I also owned the fact that if I was going to lie, then I needed to get better at it.

Neither of us spoke as Nixon drove into the underground garage of his apartment high-rise. We didn't speak during our walk to the elevators, either. We also didn't speak *in* the elevator. Neither did we speak in the hallway leading to his door. It wasn't until I noticed only two doors on either side of the hallway that I asked, "Why are there only two doors?"

"After the twentieth floor, there are only two apartments per floor," Nixon replied, short and clipped.

Well...okay, then.

Not that it mattered, because I knew that the St. James family was...uh, fortunate, but when you saw it live and in living color, well, that was something else.

Nixon unlocked his door, then stepped back to let me go in first. As soon as I was a couple of steps in, Nixon followed, then shutting and locking the door behind him, he flipped on the lights.

Holy money in the bank, Gina.

The apartment screamed wealth, taste, class, and a shitload of other words that equaled fancy. Black hardwood floors, grey with glass furniture, art on the walls...hell, even the plants looked like they cost more than my rent.

Now, stop!

Here's where you might start scoping out the place, making note of all the items that you could fence on the street. The things you couldn't afford on a pet store manager's salary, you could certainly afford if you sold off a Rembrandt, Picasso, or one of those plants.

Nevertheless, while you're enjoying the pedicures, the facials, and the Jimmy Choos, grand larceny was a *real* felony. Like, if the amount exceeded a certain limit, you'd go straight to prison. They'd skip right over local county jail time and send you. Straight. To. Prison.

Sure, you'd have the prettiest toes and softest skin there, but that glamour would fade really quickly if you didn't continue the upkeep, and who could continue the upkeep when you were too busy making shivs and fighting for your life? So, ditch the robbery plans and stick with earning a normal paycheck like the rest of America.

"You have a nice p-"

"Cut the bullshit, Lyrical," Nixon snapped, cutting off my compliment of his lovely home. "Why did you sneak out of your house and lie about a last-minute trip?"

Well, my mother didn't raise a coward, contrary to my disappearing act on Saturday morning. So, I turned to face the gorgeous, sexy, angry man, then disclosed just how high my level of crazy went, and-*scary for him*-it went rather high.

I threw my hands up in the air, then let them slap down against my sides for dramatic effect. "Because I'm crazy, Nixon," I confessed. "Because I'm shaped like a pear with no tits, a flabby tummy, a huge ass, thighs that rub together, and I'm pretty sure I suck in bed."

Nixon's eyebrows chased his hairline in a look of utter shock.

Well, at least, he wasn't pissed anymore.

"First of all, you're not shaped like a pear. And even if you were, I like pears. Second, you do have tits, as I should know, since I had them in my hands and mouth before you made me put your shirt back on last night. I can't speak on the tummy or the thighs since I did my best to be a gentleman and respect your boundaries as I fucked orgasm after orgasm out of you last night. I can, however, speak on that ass of yours since it's visible, no matter what you wear. Also, it's not huge. That ass you're sporting is sexy as hell, and I'm hoping one day you'll let me slide my cock inside it."

Nixon started to walk towards me, and I suddenly felt like prey as I digested his words and willed them to be true. Most women had insecurities and knew their every flaw, but I was neurotic in addition to being insecure, so this was a crazy combo ticket that Nixon was purchasing. "Nixo-"

He advanced, and thoughts failed me as I retreated until I found myself stopped by a wall. Nixon planted a hand on either side of my head, then leaned down in my face. "And as for you sucking in bed," he whispered. "Even without the foreplay, even without the kisses, the touches, the…details, last night was still the best fuck of my life, Lyrical." My eyes soaked up his lips as they moved. "And I have every intention of doing my best to make sure that tonight exceeds last night."

"You can do so much better," I whispered, making sure to look him in the eye. If my eyes wandered anywhere else, then I was sure to jump his bones.

Nixon started placing soft kisses on my face as he said, "I can't, Lyrical. I really, really can't do better than you because there is no one better than you."

Let's-Be-A-Hussy Lyrical grabbed Insecure Lyrical by the ear, then growled, "Listen to the man. He's given you no reason to doubt him. He's given you no reason to think he's a liar. *He's* not the one who went to Minneapolis this morning."

Oh, screw it.

I threw my arms around Nixon's neck, then started attacking him with all the force of a sex-crazed fiend. Luckily for me, he threw himself into the kiss, and soon, our hands were everywhere. However, before shit could turn rated NC-17, Nixon untangled himself, escaping from my attack.

"Wait," he panted. "Wait, a second, Lyric."

He called me Lyric.

Surely, that meant that this was something more than two semi-strangers still scratching an itch, right?

I didn't want to wait, but I did anyway. "What's wrong?"

Nixon cradled my face in his hands and those deep, intense, sweet hazel eyes of his looked so serious when he said, "Tonight, I get you naked with the lights on, Lyric." My eyes widened, but he didn't let me hide. "Tonight, I get you completely naked with the lights on while I caress your body, taste your skin, suck on your tits, and eat your pussy." *Jesus, this man had some great dirty talk.* "I get to watch your entire body cum, not just your face. I get to watch my dick stretch your pussy open, baby. I get to watch your ass bounce as I fuck you, and your tits shake as you ride me. Alright?"

This was it.

We'd only known each other a freakin' week. We'd only met up three times. We were virtual strangers. Nonetheless, Nixon was still asking me to surrender all my insecurities and just be with him; to just be with him and enjoy the moment. No crazy, no expectations, no stress, no anything...just pleasure.

Could I do it?

Hell yeah, I could.

Last night had been phenomenal, even without all the extras. So, now that he was throwing in those extras, I couldn't even begin to imagine how great tonight was going to be. I just had to trust it-trust *him.*

I took a deep breath, and from the bottom of my heart, I said the truest thing that I'd ever said. "You can do whatever you want to me, Nixon."

He groaned, and it was like my words were too much to handle. "Don't say shit like that, Lyric. I'm fine with baby steps."

"To hell with baby steps," I said, my voice sounding like it was totally onboard with my body. "I want you to fuck me like you're going to get charged at the end of the night."

"Jesus Christ," he hissed through gritted teeth.

Suddenly, I realized how unfair I'd been to this man, and I wanted to make up for it. My hands went for the buttons and zipper on his jeans, and my knees were already on the floor before he knew what was happening.

I looked up, and his perfect face was so full of hope that I almost laughed. We hadn't gotten to this last night, what with all my crazy issues and all, so this was something that I really, really wanted to give him. Still, I also didn't want him to get his hopes up too high since I was realistic about my sexual talents, or their lack of.

"I'm going to do my best to give you the best blow job you've ever had, Nixon."

He groaned as he lost his hands in my hair. "Baby, you don't have-"

Too late.

His protest was silenced, then replaced by a hiss as I wrapped my hand around his dick as far as I could, then leaned forward to swallow him whole.

"Holy fuck," he moaned as his hands tightened in my hair.

I did my best to relax my throat muscles and not strangle myself on his cock, but the dude was packing some pretty impressive equipment. My sore body this morning had been proof of that and then some.

Remembering myself, I shook off all thoughts, except the one to do my absolute best to bring him to pleasure. I sucked, licked, nibbled, and swallowed him like I was auditioning for my first porn video. I let the vibrations from my moans dance along his cock, and I put breathing on the back burner just so that Nixon could fuck my face.

Before long, Nixon had hit his breaking point. "Lyric, baby, I'm going to cum. So, if you don-*fuck.*"

I upped my tempo until Nixon was erupting in my mouth, and I gulped that shit down like a seasoned pro. In fact, I kept his cock in my mouth until I had licked him completely clean.

When I was finally done, I looked up rather pleased with myself, and then Nixon said, "Marry me, Lyric. For the love of God, marry me."

CHAPTER 18

Nixon ~
Walking into my apartment after a long Monday suddenly felt lonely, rather than relaxing, and I imagined that had something to do with missing Lyric.

She'd kept true to her word Saturday night, and she had let me do all the things that I'd wanted to do on Friday to her. By the time that the sun had come up on Sunday, there hadn't been an inch of her body that I hadn't explored. I had touched, tasted, and fucked her everywhere.

The night had been perfect.

Lyric had even stayed to have breakfast, then we'd hung out a little bit before she'd said that she had to get home and do her Sunday chores before her workweek started. I had been reluctant to let her go, but since she'd said that she was going home and not Minneapolis, I figured that I had made great leaps of progress with her. We had even exchanged phone numbers, which I had considered a huge win.

Nevertheless, now, walking into my apartment, I realized how much I wished that I was walking into her apartment or have her here waiting for me.

I dropped my briefcase on the sofa, then headed towards my bedroom to change out of my work clothes. I wanted to pretend like I could go on with life as usual before I pulled my phone out to call her like a lovesick puppy.

Once I went from suit to jeans and t-shirt, I padded my bare feet to the kitchen to see what I could whip up for dinner, and I had my phone in my hand, ready to dial Lyric, when there was a knock at my door. The sound had me feeling like a thirteen-year-old girl that was passing her school crush in the hallway. That's how many butterflies had taken over my gut at the thought that Lyrical could be here.

Jesus, if Lincoln and Jackson could see me now.

I damn near skipped to the front door, but when I pulled it open, it wasn't Lyric on the other side. I blinked a couple of times, wondering if the vision was real, and when I realized that it was, I asked, "What are you doing here?"

Rude? Yeah. Still, what in the hell?

"Really, Nixon," Dina muttered. "Is that any way to greet your guests?"

Probably not, but what in the fuck was Dina Rivers doing here?

I snapped out of my shock, then tried to invoke some of the manners that my parents had taught me. "I'm sorry, Dina. I was…just surprised, is all," I said, apologizing.

She seemed placated as she asked, "Well, aren't you going to let me in?"

For fuck what?

"Uh, yeah…sorry," I mumbled as I stepped aside, so that she could enter.

I watched her as she glanced around, taking in the apartment, though I wasn't sure why. She'd been here before when we'd been seeing each other, and it wasn't like anything had changed, and then she said as much.

"Looks like nothing's changed."

I gave my apartment a quick glance before my eyes found hers. "Nope," I agreed. "I'm not much for decorating and shit, so…everything's pretty much the same as since the last time that you were here."

"Hmm," was her only reply as she continued to look around.

Finally, at the end of my patience-because I *really* wanted to call Lyric-I asked, "What are you doing here, Dina?"

I didn't think that I was being rude, but what I'd told Jackson was true; I hadn't given this woman a second thought in years. What we'd had back then had been a casual fuck and nothing more. So, yeah, I was surprised as hell that she was here.

She finally turned her attention to me, cocking her head. "I'm not sure if you know or not, but I ran into your mother a few days ago, and…well, I got a divorce and moved back to town," she stated, and I couldn't have cared less.

I stuck my hands in my pockets, then remained standing by the door. "I'm sorry to hear about your divorce. It always sucks when two people find themselves at that final choice," I replied, suddenly realizing that Jackson had probably been right about Dina's intentions.

"Well, it's my fault," she bristled. "I settled, and I knew that I was settling. I should have had more patience to wait out something better."

Uhm, okay.

What the hell was I supposed to say to that?

Before I could comment or ask her to leave, she continued, "I figured you've probably sowed all your wild oats these past couple of years and might finally be ready for something more serious, Nixon."

Well. Fuck. Me.

Granted, she was right. However, too bad for her, that something serious that I wanted, I wanted with Lyrical.

Damn, this was going to suck.

"Dina, look," I started. "I know we go way back, and we've always gotten along well, but…well, I've already met someone who's made me want serious, and I absolutely adore the woman. She's amazing."

Dina couldn't conceal the shock that ran across her perfectly made-up face, and even without the makeup, Dina Rivers was a beautiful woman. She stood at five-foot-ten-inches with legs for days. She also had platinum blonde hair, sea-blue eyes, and a face constructed out of class and grace. Her body was made up of both original and store-bought parts, but all put together, it made for a lovely package.

She quickly got control over her facial expressions, then did her best to sound casual. "So, are you telling me that The Great Nixon St. James is in love?"

In love?

Probably not. I mean, I'd only known Lyrical going on two weeks, so it was way too soon to profess love, even if I had asked her to marry me several times Saturday night. No. I was somewhere in between liking her a hell of a whole lot and love.

That being said, I knew that I wasn't scared to fall in love with her at a later date, and I had every intention of doing so. However, I knew if I said anything short of being absolutely in love with Lyrical right now, Dina would take that as a challenge, and Lyrical didn't have any competition. This wasn't a game to be won, and if it were, Lyric was clearly the champion.

"Incredible, I know," I answered her. "Proof right there that God does exist, and miracles happen every day."

Dina shrugged off her jacket, and it gave me pause. I'd just told her that I was in love with someone else, so why would she need to take off her jacket and make herself at home?

Then I got a look at her outfit, and I had to hand it to the woman; she had come prepared. Regardless, the skin-tight dress did nothing for me. I already knew what she had underneath it, and I'd already had it. If it hadn't been good enough to lock me down years ago, I had serious doubts that-with or without Lyrical in the picture-it wasn't good enough to lock me down now.

"How are Lincoln and Jackson?" Before I could answer she went on, "I saw Jackson with your mother that day I ran into her, but he wasn't being very social."

If she only knew.

"They're both fine, Dina," I said, sticking to the short answer. I wanted this woman gone, but for the sake of our history, I'd give her a few more minutes to save face and walk out willingly.

She started making her way towards me as her fingertips danced across the back of the sofa. "You know, Nixon," she said smoothly, her voice velvety and practiced. "I'm wondering just how serious you are about this girl. I mean, you say you love her, but you're not engaged or married. Why is that?"

I had to grit my teeth. My first instinct was to tell her that it was none of her damn business, but I didn't want to draw her into an argument, prolonging her stay. I figured the sooner that I answered her, the sooner she'd get the hint and leave. So, I told her the truth, praying that this would be the end of it.

"I've asked her to marry me several times..."-Saturday night was proof of that-"...but she keeps telling me I'm moving too fast. She'd prefer a real wedding to eloping to Las Vegas." Okay, that last part was a lie. Still, the asking Lyric to marry me several times was the actual truth.

"Maybe she just doesn't want to marry you, Nixon," Dina countered. "I mean, you are rather difficult to deal with sometimes."

"I was only difficult to deal with because I refused to let you take our relationship further than what it was," I reminded her coolly. "Trust me when I tell you that my girl handles me perfectly."

Dina bristled a bit before saying, "Well, I can see you've clearly moved on."

I gave her a terse nod. "I have, Dina. I'm in love for the first time in my life. and there's nothing I won't do for that woman." I refused to give Dina Lyrical's name because I didn't want to give her anything that she could use to manipulate the situation.

She plastered on her fakest smile, then asked, "Well, before I take off and leave you to be in love, do you mind if I use your restroom really quick? I just want to freshen up before I go meet my client for our business dinner."

The alarm bells should have rung loud and clear in my mind, but they didn't. My hackles should have risen at the mention of a business dinner, because as far as I could recall, Dina hadn't worked, and she was the type of woman to bleed her ex-husband dry to maintain that lack of responsibility. Still, all the warning bells remained quiet. So, what did I do?

"Sure, help yourself. You remember where it is, right?"

"Thanks, Nixon," she cooed. "You're the best."

Turned out that I wasn't quite that good at being the best.

CHAPTER 19

Lyrical ~
My palms were sweaty, and I felt ridiculous. Nonetheless, I stood in front of Nixon's door another few minutes before gathering up the courage to knock.

Saturday night had been beyond what I had ever imagined sex could be. Nixon had worshipped every inch of my skin, and each word that he had whispered, every kiss that he had placed, every tenderly violent act that he had committed had made me feel beautiful, wanted, and desired.

Even now, I wasn't sure how he had managed it, but I'd only felt embarrassed a couple of times that night. The rest of the time, I'd been so lost in the pleasure that he'd been creating around me that I hadn't had time to worry about flabby skin or dimpled thighs.

The first time had been when I had climbed over him to ride him. The second that I'd sat my weight across his waist, I had worried that I might be too heavy. However, the second that Nixon had sensed the change in me, he had grabbed me by my hips, then had used every rippling, sweaty, strong muscle in his arms to lift me, then slam me back down on his cock. Not only had he blown my mind with the pleasure from seating himself so deep inside of me, but he'd also proven to me that my weight was nothing for him.

The second time embarrassment had started to rear its ugly head had been when I'd just been coming down off an orgasmic high, and Nixon had nudged the head of his dick against the opening of my ass. Never having had anal sex before, my entire body had turned bright red with embarrassment and anxiousness.

I had started worrying about the logistics of how it would all work when Nixon covered my back with his chest, then had whispered in my ear, "Trust me, Lyric. Trust me, and if I let you down on this, I'll never ask you to trust me ever again." I still hadn't been sure, but then he had upped the ante by adding, "I dream of fucking you up the ass, baby. Don't ruin my dreams because of fear. I promise to make you love it."

So, I had trusted him, letting him do his worst. At first it had been painful, and I had wondered who in their right mind would ever want to engage in something so painful, dirty, and sinful. However, then the pain had given way to a different sensation that eventually had given way to unimaginable pleasure. By the end of the night, I had begged Nixon to violate me everywhere on my body, and the man had done his best to deliver.

Now, stop!

This was the part where you might want to ditch your birth control to get pregnant and trap him into marriage.

DO. NOT. DO. THIS.

If you went and trap this wonderful man, then he'd be forced to marry you, but start to resent you over time, thus causing him to cheat on you. Then, because of the insecurities that a team of psychologists couldn't fix, you'd end up murdering him and his mistress at their hotel room where there were cameras, instead of plotting out a more carefully crafted double-murder where you didn't get caught.

Murder was usually a guaranteed life sentence, but double-murder? Yeah, just…do not trap him. Let him fall in love with you naturally.

Snapping myself out of my thoughts, I decided that I'd been standing in the hallway, looking like a tool long enough. I squared my shoulders as if I was preparing to go into battle, then knocked on the door. Nixon must have been standing next to it because the door swung open not a few seconds later.

He looked down at me, and he looked…confused. "Oh, hey…uhm, I wasn't expecting you," he uttered, sounding a bit lost in thought.

It wasn't the enthusiasm that I'd been hoping for, but it wasn't a door slammed in my face, either. "I'm sorry," I immediately replied. "I probably should have called. Are you busy?"

Nixon shook his head a little, clearing away the confusion on his face, then blurted out, "No. I'm not busy."

I stood there as my anxiety was taking off at rocket speed. "Can I come in?"

"What?" His brows shot upward, and he really looked out of sorts. "Of course. Yeah. Come in, come in," he muttered as he stepped aside, allowing me entrance into his apartment.

I walked in, and the first thing that I noticed was a jacket that appeared to be feminine lying across the back of his couch. My heart started to beat frantically, and I could feel emptiness where my insides used to be.

Don't jump to conclusions…Don't jump to conclusions…Don't jump to conclusions.

I mean, the man had a mother, right? Maybe his parents were visiting him this evening, and that's why he seemed all scattered brain. He just wasn't ready to introduce me to his parents, and I'd gone and placed him in an awkward position.

Nonetheless, I wasn't going to play any games. I mean, he couldn't say all the things that he'd said Saturday night and not expect me to think that we were exclusive, right? Sure, we were nowhere near a serious commitment, but the man had proposed several times Saturday, so that had to mean something.

I turned to face him, then pointblank asked him, "Do you have company? Am I interrupting anything?"

He stepped to me, then placed his hands on my shoulders. "Not exactly," he replied. "But you're not int-"

Whatever Nixon had been about to say was cut short when a very stunning, built, and flawless-looking blonde walked out of the hallway, wearing nothing but a matching, skimpy, red-laced bra and panty set that looked like it cost more than a car. She also came with perfectly matching red fuck-me heels. She looked like she belonged on the centerfold in any men's magazine in the world.

"Oh, Nixon, darling," she sing-songed. "I can't wait any longer, lover." Her eyes shot to mine, and she let out the most feminine shocked gasp that I'd ever heard. "Oh, my God. Oh, I'm so embarrassed." She looked back over at Nixon. "Nixon, honey, why didn't you tell me you were expecting someone."

I noticed that in her shocked embarrassment, she hadn't bothered to shield herself in the least. Granted, why should she? She had a perfect fucking body.

Nixon's hand dropped from my shoulders as he turned to face her. *"What?"*

"I better leave," I mumbled, numb and yet feeling like a complete fool.

Now, stop!

Here's the part where the level of your pain and humiliation was so high that you didn't care if you went to jail. Your first instinct would probably be to storm over to the perfect female creation, then beat the snot out of her, but don't. Because let me tell you, women like that had an attorney on retainer, and not only would she press charges, but she'd also sue you.

You also couldn't afford to lose what little you had over a man-*any* man. Besides, she wasn't the cheater. Oh, you'd love to place the blame on her because if it's her fault, then your poor man was innocently outmaneuvered by a master manipulator, so you won't feel like such a weakling when you forgave him later, because women always want to forgive the bastards.

You didn't want to believe that you weren't enough. You wanted to believe that it had nothing to do with his love for you. You wanted it to be *her* fault.

Still, it wasn't.

It was his fault, and his fault alone, and any man that was going to spend all night inside you on Saturday, and then have a woman-*who looked nothing like you*-half-naked in his house, only two days later, wasn't worth the jailtime.

No man was worth the jail time.

I brushed past Nixon towards the door, but I wasn't even two steps in when I felt him grab my arm. "Lyric, wait a sec-"

"Nixon, who is this woman?" the perfect female asked.

Nixon turned to her but didn't release my arm. "Are you fucking kidding me right now, Dina?"

Dina.

Her name was Dina, and it fit her perfectly.

"What's going on, Nixon," she asked. "Who is she?"

The more outraged that she sounded, the sorrier that I felt for her; for both of us. Nixon St. James was playing us both, but it seemed like he'd been playing her longer, and I really felt sorry for her. It sucked to be played for a fool, I ought to know.

"I'm no one," I told her, hoping that I could get out of here without being subjected to any serious drama. The sooner that I could get out of here, the sooner I could get home and fall apart.

Nixon ignored her questions, then looked back down at me. "Lyrical, it's not what you think. She-"

I hated that phrase: 'It's not what you think'.

It had to be the biggest insult to someone's intelligence when you told them that.

"Really? Because it looks like I interrupted a night of fun and excitement for you and Dina," I retorted, trying to hold onto my hurt emotions and temper.

"Lyric-"

"Goddamn it, Nixon," Dina snapped "Are you *cheating* on me?"

That was my cue.

I shook off Nixon's hold on my arm, then ran out of his apartment like a coward.

CHAPTER 20

Nixon ~
What in the fuck was happening?

I heard the door shut behind Lyric, and as much as I loathed to leave Dina alone in my apartment, I knew that I had to go after her. So, I grabbed Dina's jacket off the couch, then threw it at her. As it slapped against her chest, I yelled, "You have two minutes to get your shit and get the fuck out of my house before they never find your body, Dina!"

"Are you serious?" she asked, actually offended. "Let's talk-"

I had one hand already on the doorknob. "If you've ruined what I have with that woman who just left here, I will fucking *ruin* you, Dina."

I didn't bother to wait around for her response. I flung the front door open, then ran down the hallway to chase Lyric down. The elevator doors were shutting, but I could still see Lyric frantically pushing the buttons through the closing gap.

"Lyrical!" I yelled, but it was too late, the elevator started to descend.

Luckily, the stairwell wasn't too far away, so I slammed open the door, then hit those stairs running. I ran down twenty-five flights of stairs, and the only things that kept me going were adrenaline and fear. If Lyrical made it out of the lobby, then I was going to lose her. I also didn't care that I was barefooted because there was no way that I wasn't running after her.

Christ, this couldn't be happening.

It'd been years since I'd last seen Dina, much less slept with her, so I never would have thought that Jackson's warning deserved any consideration. It wasn't like I'd been a great guy to her back then. Hell, I wasn't even that great of a guy now.

What Dina and I had back then had been very casual. I hadn't ever treated her like a girlfriend or a potential wife. We fucked. End of story. Regardless, I supposed that woman scorned thing was true because that shitshow back at my apartment was all jealousy and unwarranted revenge. It didn't take a genius to figure out that Dina had probably been planning on laying out on my bed in her lingerie, hoping to entice me. However, when she'd heard a woman's voice in the living room, she had decided to change up her plans and fuck my life up.

I also wasn't a complete idiot. This shit looked bad, and I realized that. I also knew that the scene upstairs looked worse for someone with Lyric's deep seeded self-esteem issues. Now, while in my eyes, Lyric was perfect, I could only imagine what she'd thought looking at a perfectly built Dina Rivers. It didn't matter that Dina was fake as hell, either. Some women just couldn't help but compare themselves to other women, and with Lyric feeling like she was shaped like a pear and undesirable, I knew that, in this moment, Lyric was convincing herself that I belonged with someone that looked like Dina.

After what felt like a lifetime, I finally pushed open the stairwell doors, then raced towards the elevators. I looked up to see the numbers had hit the lobby already, so then I started scanning the room, then noticed Lyrical striding towards the front doors of the lobby. She'd had her right hand on the door handle when I reached her, grabbed her arm, then dragged her into the nearest corner.

I had to give it to her; the girl was scrappy. She was fighting my hold with everything that she had. "Let me go, Nixon," she seethed, her eyes blazing with pure unadulterated hate.

"Not until you've heard me out, Lyrical," I snapped. I could admit that it looked bad, but I deserved a chance to explain. She couldn't just assume the worst, then storm out of my life.

All my life, I'd never given much thought to the women that I'd slept with because I'd always been upfront about my intentions. I hadn't ever led them on, and I had always tried to be respectful, if not detached. Dina had been no different, even though I had slept with her longer than my other hookups. I'd never been afraid of a woman dumping me or walking away from me because I'd never cared before, so this was a first and a last, I hoped.

Still, Lyrical was unpredictable and...well, crazy.

Trying to still yank her arm out of my hold, she snapped back, "I don't need to hear you out, Nixon. It's clear to anyone with eyes what that was, and if you think I'm going to stand down here and argue with you while you have a naked woman up in your apartment, you are sorely mistaken."

"She was *not* naked," I said, correcting her, though, to Lyric, that distinction was probably irrelevant. However, to me, I felt like it was something that I needed to clarify.

Lyrical shook her head. "You think that matters?!" she yelled, confirming that it was indeed irrelevant to her. *'Fine.* I'm not going to stand down here and argue with you while you have a *half-naked* woman up in your apartment."

"Lyric, don't do this," I begged as it dawned on me just how resolute her voice sounded. "I'll go upstairs and get rid of Dina, but please hear me out. Let me explain."

"Explain what?" she growled. "What's there to explain?"

"That it's not what it looks like!" I yelled, feeling desperate and panicky.

I watched as Lyrical took a deep breath, doing her best to calm down. I was guessing that she didn't want to end up on YouTube any more than I did. Nonetheless, I'd gladly end up on the internet if it meant that we had worked shit out.

When she finally got herself under control, she said, "I'm going home, Nixon. If you want to discuss this some more, then you can come by later after you've...after you've handled your business with Dina."

My stomach dipped.

I didn't trust her words.

I felt like I'd lose her forever if I let her out of my sight right now. Still, what choice did I have? "Okay," I replied. "I'll be there ten minutes after you get home."

Lyric left me standing in the lobby as she stormed out of the building, and something told me to just go after her as is, but I didn't. Instead, I turned to head back to my place to at least grab some goddamn shoes before I chased her across town. Unfortunately for me, when I turned to rush towards the elevator, I saw it ding open, then Dina walking out.

I knew that I had a violent temper, but I'd never felt such rage against a woman before in my life. Still, even as angry as I was, I knew that I couldn't kill her. Too many witnesses, for one, and they wouldn't let Lyrical live with me in prison, for two.

"Nixon-"

I didn't stop on my way to the elevator. "Stay away from me, Dina," I called back to her. "If you ever come near me ever again, you *will* be sorry."

Not caring about her one fucking bit, I stepped into the elevator, then pushed the button that would take me to my floor with more force than was necessary.

Why, why, why?

Why would The Fates do this to me? Was it payback for every woman that I'd never taken seriously? Because I mean...c'mon, falling for a crazy person should be karma enough if you asked me. I already knew that my life was going be riddled with colorful moments being with someone like Lyrical, so I didn't need this trial-by-fire bullshit.

I already knew that Lyric was crazy.

I already knew that she wouldn't take my shit.

I already knew that Lincoln was going to have to be on retainer for her, too.

I did not need Dina fucking Rivers popping into my life as a goddamn test.

I stepped out of the elevator when the doors opened to my floor, then I raced to my front door, flinging it open. I quickly found a pair of shoes, slipped them on, grabbed my wallet and keys, then rushed back downstairs.

When the elevator hit the garage floor, I practically ran to my car, and I was out of the garage in under a minute, and the entire drive to Lyric's apartment was made in a complete state of panic.

Lyric wasn't like a lot of women. She didn't care about my money, my looks, or my family's pedigree. A lot of women would blow this off in favor of benefitting from all those three things, but not Lyrical. Lyric was more likely to tell me to go eat a dick as she'd be to ask me to borrow five dollars. So, I couldn't blind her with diamonds or furs. I couldn't seduce her with good looks or charm, which, admittedly, I was short on the charm part because I had a brooding disposition, but still.

I was driving like a maniac to her place as I prayed that begging and logic would prevail. However, how did begging and logic prevail when you were dealing with someone who was prideful and crazy?

Fortunately or unfortunately, life had come easy to me for the past few years. I hadn't had to fight for anything or anyone in a long time, and I sure as hell had never fought for a woman before. So, I was super out of my element, and I wasn't so insecure that I couldn't admit it.

I pulled up to the curb in front of my building and the feeling was an odd one. I wasn't here to inspect the property or evict a tenant. I wasn't here to showcase the place or meet with the new building manager. I was here to fight for the only woman that had ever inspired that out of me.

I got out of the car, then briefly wondered if I should have called Linc to have him on standby. As pissed and hurt as Lyrical was, who knew what awaited me in her apartment. She probably had a set of steak knives that were going to be aimed at my head the second that she opened the door.

I got onto the elevator, and the ride was the longest in history. I did my best to not fidget, but the other people in the elevator could tell that I was on edge, and how did I know that you ask?

I could tell when the little girl with the blonde pigtails told her mother, "I think that man's scared, Momma."

No shit.

CHAPTER 21

Lyrical ~
I didn't want to go to my apartment and wait for Nixon. I didn't want to see him, much less listen to whatever lame ass excuse that he had planned to follow 'It's not what it looks like'.

However, the funny thing about it all?

I wasn't even sure what I was feeling right now. My heart was telling me that it was broken while my mind was telling me to be practical since Nixon and I had never clarified that this thing that we'd been doing was exclusive. As for my anger? My anger was telling me to go back there, then beat that woman until she no longer looked like perfection. It was also telling me to cut off Nixon's dick, then feed it to him until he choked to death.

Christ, how I wanted to listen to my anger.

Luckily, pride stepped up and was telling me to get it together. It was also pointing out that I should really be quite tired of humiliating myself in front of Nixon St. James by now. I also totally decided to ignore my mind when it kept trying to interject that Nixon and I had never established exclusivity between us. Besides, it wasn't like Nixon didn't already know that I was crazy. So, if I decided to go ahead and ignore my broken heart, mind, and pride, and just feed into my anger and go balls-out on the fuckface, he shouldn't be surprised, right?

It was only eight minutes later when there was a knock on my door. I seriously contemplated not answering, but if there was one thing that I knew to be true, it was that people needed closure. You needed the grand finale, or else you ended up with pockets of self-doubt later on down the road. Now, while I might not have an issue living with pockets of insanity every now and again, regret sucked, and so I tried to avoid it as much as possible.

I answered the door, and a very haggard-looking Nixon St. James stood before me. At least, he put on some shoes, which was a good thing since he looked like he ran here. I stepped back, giving him enough room to walk into my apartment, even though what I really wanted to do was slam the door in his overly-handsome face.

When the door shut behind me, Nixon turned around, and he looked like he had so much to say but had suddenly forgotten how to speak English. He looked lost, and I hated that. I hated it because he actually looked like *he* was the victim in all this.

The asshole.

"Lyrical, I-"

I put my hand up to stop him. I knew that I'd been the one who'd told him that he could come over to explain, but I really just didn't feel like hearing his bullshit. Plus, because I had deep seeded issues, even if there was an innocent explanation for all of this, seeing firsthand the kind of women that he got involved with was a real eye opener.

How in the hell did a pear compete with a shiny, delicious, ruby-red apple? Everyone loved apples. They were so loved that there was even a saying coined after them: 'An apple a day keeps the doctor away'. Have you ever heard any snazzy sayings about pears? No? Yeah…well, I hadn't, either.

"Nixon, can I be real with you?" I asked, even though his answer was nonconsequential since I was going to say what I had to say, regardless.

Nixon let out a deep sigh. "Have you ever been anything else?"

What a fucking twat.

I mean, he was the one that had fucked up here, not me. So, you'd think that the least he could do was watch his words.

I decided to ignore his comment because…well, let's face it, it hadn't really been a question, and I *had* been about to go full-blown psycho on him. However, my pride rose from the ashes of my broken self-esteem, then whispered quietly in my head, "This will be like the hundredth time you've humiliated yourself in front of this man. Don't do it again, Lyrical. *Don't. Do. It.*"

Then the pressure started building behind my eyes, and I could feel my nose tingle, and that just couldn't be. My pride was right, and Nixon's comment of 'Have you ever been anything else' was enough for me to pull out my hidden supply of cold, cool, and calculated.

"Nixon, let me be frank with you," I started, ignoring the tick in his jaw. It was probably due to how unaffected my voice sounded, but I didn't care. "It really doesn't matter what you have planned to say. No words, explanations, or excuses can create time travel and make what just happened not happen. I'm also finding that two weeks of knowing a person doesn't exactly equal an epic heartbreak just because I wasn't the only one. So, I-"

Nixon was up in my face before I knew what he was about, snatching me by my arm, shaking me a little, and I gotta say, I wasn't expecting that. "You *are* the only one, Lyrical," he snapped. "You've been the *only* one since the second that you accused me of cheating on Randall with Lincoln. I haven't been with or wanted to be with anyone else since I met you."

Now, stop!

This might be the part where you cave; where your heart overrules your mind and screams to believe him. However, did you know why it did that? It did that because heartbreak was painful as hell. It hurts so much that you'd give almost anything to not feel the anguish that you were feeling. Your heart convinces you that it was all a big misunderstanding, so that you could look yourself in the mirror every day, even though, deep down, you know the real truth.

So, you don't cave.

You don't cave because your mind explains to your heart that we can get through this heartbreak once, but we're not sure if we can get through it twice, and if a man cheats once, he'll cheat again.

I tried to laugh out an evil cackle like they did in the movies, but it just sounded like I was choking on my own spit. However, once I got that shit under control, I was able to pull off a respectable scoff, saying, "Says the man who had a half-naked goddess walking out of his bedroom." I yanked my arm out of Nixon's grasp. "Jesus Christ, Nixon. You must really think me stupid. *Or desperate.*"

His jaw ticked again, but I didn't care how pissed he was. "I can explain tha-"

"Oh, I'm sure you can," I sneered, instead of trying for the evil cackle again. "Let's see, she's a model that got lost in your building, and she mistook your friendly help for something more. Or maybe she's your sister, but she's just friendlier than most. Or she's a crazy ex that's stalking you and climbed in your bedroom window, unbeknownst to you. Or-"

"That's enough, Lyric," Nixon bit out. "Are you going to listen to what I have to say or not?"

I cocked my head at him, pretty proud of myself that I wasn't a blubbering mess right now, then laid out the absolute truth of the situation. "Here's the thing, Nixon," I replied. "It doesn't matter which one of those scenarios are right, if any. It doesn't matter because it's not like we were in a relationship or anything like that."

His face paled a little bit. "Lyr-"

"We've only known each other for a couple of weeks, and we've only fucked like twice," I recalled coldly. "It's not like you were my boyfriend, and I had all exclusive rights or something."

Nixon's face went from pale to a furious red, and I felt like Furious Red should be a legit shade on the color prism because it looked extremely colorful on Nixon's pissed off face. "Are you fucking kidding me right now?"

I shrugged a shoulder, sticking with Cool Lyrical. "Well, I mean, sure I was upset at first. I think it was the unexpected shock, you know. But once I had time to think about it…well, you aren't my boyfriend, Nixon. You never were, so it's totally cool if we see other people. It's my fault for not calling ahead to let you know I was stopping by anyway."

Nixon stood there, giving me the dirtiest look imaginable, and then he was able to do what I hadn't been. The bastard cackled evilly as he said, "Bull-fucking-shit, Lyrical." He grabbed me by my arm again. "You think I don't know what you're doing?" He didn't let me answer. "I know *exactly* what you're doing."

I didn't bother to try to break free from his hold because we both knew that he could out-muscle me. "Oh, yeah? What am I doing?"

"You're playing like what we've done doesn't mean anything, so that you're not hurt by the truth that you already believe inside that beautiful, neurotic, whacked-out head of yours," he hissed in my face.

How dare he bring up my mental defects.

"So, then what's the story, Nixon?" I asked, not really wanting to know because the man had hit the nail on the head. "If the story in my whacked-out head is false, then what's the truth?"

Nixon's gorgeous face contorted into a vicious snarl, and I couldn't lie, it was kind of hot. "That fucking bitc-*woman* in my apartment was someone who I briefly dated a couple of years back." I'd already known that I wasn't going to like his explanation, but the pang still hit hard at hearing that he'd been involved with that bit of feminine perfection at one point in time. "She got married last year, and she stopped by to tell me that she was divorced and that she's moved back to town. She was hoping that I was ready to settle down. Preferably with her."

"And you insisted the conversation take place with her dressed in her lingerie?"

"No," he snapped out. "I told her I was dating you, and she asked if she could use the restroom before she left. I didn't think anything of it and told her yes." Nixon ran a hand through his chocolate tresses as he let out a low growl. "She must have heard us talking and decided to put on that ridiculous show, hoping to break us up. I don't know, Lyric. But I *didn't* have a half-naked woman at my place. If I had, you think I would have let you come inside?"

I hated that his story sounded plausible. I hated the fact that some women were capable of that kind of deceit and drama. Worse than that, though? I hated that I wanted to believe him.

Those women? Those women that were so in love, or so desperate for affection that they jumped at the chance to believe the first excuse to leave the betrayer's mouth? Yeah. I didn't want to be one of those women. I didn't want to be blinded by love. I didn't want to be a fool.

I planted my hands on my hips as I cocked my head. "And it only took you eight minutes to come up with that story?" I smirked. "I'm impressed."

CHAPTER 22

Nixon ~
I was pissed.

I was so fucking pissed, and the only thing keeping me from tearing the place apart was the fact that this woman, the same one that had given herself over to me Saturday night, had walked into my apartment to find a hot woman wearing nothing but lingerie coming out of my hallway as if we'd had a night of debauchery scheduled.

I knew how bad it looked, and for that reason alone, I was doing my best not to flip the fuck out at Lyrical calling me a liar to my face. In all my thirty-three years of life, I'd been a lot of things, but never a liar. I didn't lie; there was no point in it. Sure, it made me appear like a dick sometimes, but in my opinion, the truth was more important than what people thought of me. I was trying to recall the last time that someone had insulted my integrity to my face, and I couldn't come up with a time. I couldn't remember the last time that someone had insulted me to this degree.

My back straightened, and I could feel the anger boiling in my veins. I also wasn't doing anything to hide it from my face as I towered over Lyrical, pissed as fuck. "It's not a story I made up," I seethed. "It's the fucking truth, Lyrical. She's someone I used to fuck with *years* ago, and she didn't take it well when I told her I'd moved on to a serious relationship."

The mutinous look on her face faltered a bit, but she was quick to call on her reinforcements. She shrugged her damn shoulder again as if she didn't have a care in the world. "I don't really care if your story is true or not, Nixon. The fact remains that we've only known each other for a couple of weeks. There's nothing wrong with seeing other people."

That was the second time that she'd said that shit, and it was making me murderous. Hell, maybe I really was in love with her, because I couldn't imagine how I was getting this feral over her if I weren't. I could barely get the words out, but I managed through gritted teeth. "I will fuck up any man you dare bring home, Lyrical. So, I suggest you don't."

Her beautiful brown eyes widened, and I could see that she hadn't been expecting that. "You…you can't just say stuff like that," she announced. "Fighting is against the law, Nixon. You'll get arrested."

Like I gave a fuck.

"Well, then I guess it's a good thing that Lincoln's a damn good criminal lawyer," I snapped.

Jesus Christ, I was pissed. I couldn't recall ever being so mad before in my life, and that was saying something, considering the temper that I had. Still, Lyrical was trying me something fierce.

She must have seemed to realize that she'd broken her aloof persona, because she quickly shook off her shock, then went back to acting like an ice princess. "Don't be ridiculous, Nixon," she huffed. "Jail isn't worth it over a casual hookup."

Forget assault on her imaginary lover, Lincoln was going to have to defend me for murder because I was about to strangle the hell out of this crazy woman for saying fucked-up shit like that. "Believe me when I tell you that *nothing* about you is casual, Lyric," I said acidly. "But that aside, I'm not lying about how Dina ended up in my apartment. I'm not a fucking liar."

She narrowed her eyes at me, finally getting rid of her cool-girl act. "Even if your story is true, Nixon, that doesn't mean you need to explain yourself to me," she snapped. "Like I said, this is just a casual hook-"

Fuck that shit.

I wasn't going to stand here and listen to her tell me how acceptable it was to have another woman in my apartment. I was not going to stand here and let her downplay our connection because, believe me, we had one, even if she didn't want to acknowledge it right now.

My arm snaked out, and grabbing her by her arm, I pulled her towards me, then flung her crazy ass over the back of the couch. She was wearing a skirt, and I just knew—*just knew*—The Good Lord had done me this favor to make up for Satan steering Dina in my direction. He was a good Lord after all.

"Nixon, what are you doing?" Lyrical gasped.

I had her skirt flipped up over her waist with one hand positioned flat in the middle of her back, keeping her in place. My other hand was working my button and zipper. "I'm proving to you that this thing between us is anything *but* casual."

"Oh, my God, are you insane?" she cried out, adding more gasps to her theatrics.

"Yes," I bit back. "I am, now that you mention it. And do you want to know why? Because you make me fucking crazy, Lyric. You are constantly driving me out of my goddamn mind. So, congratulations, you win. You win my sanity, my heart, my soul…all of it."

"Nixon…" she rasped.

I didn't want to hear it.

I just didn't.

Lyrical thought that I was bullshitting, but I wasn't. She was seriously driving me out of my goddamn mind, and I didn't know how to deal with it. I wasn't good with uncertainty, and shit was always uncertain where this woman was concerned.

The second my dick was freed, I yanked Lyric's panties down until they got trapped around the middle of her thighs, then I slid my cock between her ass cheeks, and sure enough, when the head of my dick rubbed against her opening, it was already slick with need.

Casual my motherfucking ass.

I rammed my cock in hard and deep, and I ignored her scream as I started pounding into her tight, drenched, hot paradise. I couldn't stop the hiss that escaped from my lips at the feel of her. Both nights that I had spent with Lyric, I'd spent them fucking her all night long, but sliding into her always felt like the first time.

"Oh, God...Nixon..."

My hands grabbed her hips, and I was pounding into her body so hard that the couch kept moving with every thrust. I was so lost in the sensation of her tight pussy that it was hard to think or speak, but I managed. "Want to tell me again how this is casual?" I grunted.

"Nixon...*please*..."

"Please, what? Please, make you cum? Or, please, go make *Dina* cum?"

It'd been a fucked-up thing to say. It had to be the biggest asshole moment of my life, but I was pissed. Of course, that wasn't any excuse because anger didn't give anyone the right to hurt someone else's feelings. Nonetheless, Lyric was accusing me of being a liar, and saying that it was okay for us to fuck other people, so I just wanted her to put her money where her mouth was.

"Fuck you, Nixon!" she screamed. "Fuck you!"

Interesting that I noticed how she wasn't asking me to stop as she was cussing me out. "Ah, so then it *is* you that you want me to make cum, huh?"

Lyrical reached back, then her hands started pushing at my chest. She was slapping away at me, trying to get me off her. "Get off me!"

Since I wasn't a rapist, I pulled out of her immediately, then took a couple of steps back. I wasn't expecting to see what I saw when Lyrical whirled around to face me; Lyrical looked like she hated my guts.

The hate, the pain, the regret...they were consuming everything that made up those beautiful brown eyes of hers. I watched her skirt slide down over her hips as I tucked my dick back into my pants, and I ignored how my hands shook with the simple movement.

"Get out of my house, Nixon," she seethed, hate dripping from every syllable. "Get out of my house, and don't ever come back. Don't ever call or come by or...or anything." Tears started streaming down her face, and I wasn't sure if they were from pain or anger.

The full force of what I'd just done hit me as soon as her tears spilled over, and regret was like the heaviest of boulders sitting in the pit of my stomach. "Lyrica-"

"No. Fuck you, Nixon," she hissed. "You stick your dick inside me as some half-ass show of proof that what we have is serious, but then you dare to say another woman's name at the same time? Are you fucking kidding me?"

I put my hand up to try to calm her. "Look, I realized that might have been an error on my part, but-"

"Might have been?" she bit out, her eyes round with hate. Lyric shook her head, and her usually beautiful face contorted maliciously. "Whether casual or not, it doesn't matter anymore, Nixon. Whatever this is, it's over. Now, get out of my house."

Panicked was probably the word that I'd use to describe what my entire body was feeling right now. I screwed up, and I screwed up badly. We also didn't have a long history to keep her from ending this. We didn't have words of love, or any kids to keep her from just cutting her losses altogether.

"I'm going to leave, Lyric, because we're both in a bad head space right now," I told her. "But you're out of your mind if you think this is over." She went to open her mouth, but I cut her off. "I know I fucked up, but you fucked up, too. You should have given me the benefit of the doubt and not jump to the automatic conclusion that painted me as the bad guy. I'm a lot of things, Lyrical, but I'm not a fucking liar."

She raised her chin, doing her best to stare me down. "You might not be a liar, Nixon," she said, her eyes lasered in on mine. "But you're definitely a mistake. One I won't keep repeating."

Lyrical stormed back to her bedroom, not giving me a chance to claim that I wasn't.

CHAPTER 23

Lyrical ~
There was music, laughter, and conversation all around me, but I wasn't absorbing any of it. The only thing that I was absorbing was the alcohol from the beers and tequila shots.

"Look, Lyric," Rena said right after our third shot. "I get that what he did was super dickish, but you gotta take some responsibility for this crap, too."

I twisted in my barstool to gape at her. "What? You're supposed to be on my side, goddamn it."

She rolled her eyes. "I *am* on your side, Lyric. I'm *always* on your side," she assured me. "The thing is, had you given Nixon a chance to explain, it wouldn't have gotten that far."

"And you think he deserved for me to hear him out?" I scoffed. "He had a half-naked bimbo in his apartment, Rena."

Rena cocked her head at me. "Let me ask you this. Do you believe him or not about what that woman was doing there?"

Ugh.

That was the worst part of all this bullshit; I *did* believe him. I believed him, but I didn't want to. Still, I wasn't going to lie to Rena. "I do," I admitted. "I do, but I don't want to."

Rena's face was full of confused surprise when she asked, "Why the hell not?"

I downed my beer, then signaled the bartender for another round. I looked back at my best friend, then told her the absolute insecure truth of the matter. "Because I don't want to be that female, Rena."

"What fucking female?" She shook her head, then yelled at the bartender, "And another round of shots, too, please." She looked back at me, then repeated, "What fucking female?"

"The one that's so in love that she ignores the signs, Rena. *That* female," I groaned. "The female who…who sits at home, like an ignorant fool, while the man she thinks loves her is fucking around with other women behind her back. That goddamn female, Rena. *That one.*"

"Jesus Christ, Lyr, what has Nixon done to ever give you the impression that he would turn you into that kind of woman? You've only known the man…what? Three weeks?"

The bartender placed our beers and shots in front of us, and like the fine-tuned engine that our friendship was, we halted the conversation to throw back our shots before resuming making our points. After all, we were experts at drinking while solving the world's problems.

"God, Rena," I choked out pathetically. "You should have seen her. She was too perfect-looking to be real."

Rena's face softened as soon as she realized what the real issue at hand was. "Lyrical…"

"I got scared, Rena," I finally admitted out loud. "I…I think I was really falling for Nixon, and when I compared myself to…to what he's used to dating, well, how the hell am I supposed to keep his interest in the long run?"

"Oh, sweetie," she said sadly. "Then tell him that. You've always spoken your mind about anything and everything, so don't start hiding now, Lyric. Tell him the truth. Be honest, then let him decide if he wants to commit to having to reassure you forever or if he'd rather just walk away."

I took a drink of my new beer before asking, "Just like that, huh? It's just that simple?"

Rena scoffed. "Hell to the fucking no. There's nothing simple about laying yourself bare to another person, especially one who already intimidates you. I imagine it's going to be one of the hardest things you've ever done."

"Thanks," I deadpanned. "Thanks for that. So, you're saying I'm the one who needs to apologize?"

"Fuck no," she scoffed again. "He needs to apologize. He needs to apologize for the ex and for being a first-class dick. What *you* need to do is let him, because you haven't been being fair to the man. From the beginning, you've been using your insecurities as a shield against whatever he's been trying to build with you."

I twisted all the way around on my barstool, then looked out over the lounge. It was only early evening, but it was already getting crowded with preppy types and professionals that appeared to be real professionals. I imagined that this was the type of place that the St. James men would frequent and feel comfortable being at.

Rena's gaze followed mine. "I still don't know why you chose this place. These people set their drinks down on coasters, and there's not even a karaoke machine anywhere in sight."

I let out a soft laugh. "I chose this place because I was pretty sure we wouldn't run into anyone we knew," I answered. "I wanted to wallow in private, but where there was an unlimited amount of booze at my disposal."

"Well, we definitely aren't going to run into any of our people here, that's for sure," Rena retorted, her voice full of wryness.

I had a good buzz going, and I also knew that I needed to speak with Nixon. So, I was about to suggest that we leave, but then a tall, perfect-looking, platinum blonde walking in caught my eye.

Sonofabitch.

"That's her," I announced before thinking better of it. After all, this was Rena that I was talking to. The woman wasn't afraid to catch a court case.

"Who's her?" she asked, but then realization dawned as she took in my expression as I stared at Dina standing near the door, her head swiveling about, taking in the scene.

My voice caught when Dina's casual glance found me looking at her. The fucking bitch smirked, then actually had the audacity to make her way over towards us. Her expensive black heels stopped directly in front of me, and she only spared Rena a quick glance before turning her attention back on me.

"I'm sorry," she said smoothly. "I wasn't able to catch your name the last time we…uh, met."

I called on every scrap of inner pride that I had, doing my best to keep my face looking neutral and making sure that my temper stayed in check. "It's Lyrical," I replied, then added, "Dina."

The corner of her lip lifted, and her face looked perfectly haughty. "Ah, so Nixon *has* mentioned me."

Rena was as quiet as a tomb sitting next to me, but I knew that could change at any moment. "Only as he was explaining how you arrived at his apartment, pathetic and desperate to get back together," I said cheekily.

This time, her lip curled, and she looked ugly and jealous. "And I supposed you've convinced yourself to believe I wasn't there at his request? You believe I wasn't naked in his apartment for a reason?"

If I hadn't believed Nixon before, I'd believe him now. Dina's hate, jealousy, and ugliness were palpable with every word that she spoke.

"I know you weren't there at his request," I stated, firmly and confidently. "And the reason you were there was exactly as Nixon explained. It was a pathetic attempt to lure him back into a relationship with you." I cocked my head to the side. "But then was it really a relationship to begin with, or did you guys just fuck?"

"You bitch!" she shrieked, not caring about our audience.

"Perhaps," I conceded, grinning. "But at least I'm not a desperate, pathetic, rejected one."

Rena laughed beside me. "You tell her, Lyr."

Dina's face turned towards Rena, then did the one thing that she shouldn't have.

This dumb bitch got crazy with Rena Salinger.

"Why don't you mind your own goddamn business, you stupid cow!" she screeched, and pointing out her desperation must have really hit a sore spot.

Rena hopped off her barstool, causing me to hop off mine. Then as Rena narrowed her eyes at Dina, she said, "Bitch, just because we're not out in the street, doesn't mean that I won't kick your motherfucking ass."

Dina scoffed. "You think I'm scared of you?"

Rena planted her hands on her hips. "You should be," she countered, and it was then that I realized that I couldn't let my friend get in trouble over my drama with Nixon. She didn't deserve the bullshit that would come with popping Dina in the face.

Now, stop!

This was the part where you might want to just pop Dina one, but you don't. You don't because you know, deep down, that you've won. Nixon didn't want her. He wanted *you*. So, you become the bigger person because fighting was for the uncouth.

However, that was my best friend that Dina was fucking with.

I turned towards my best friend, then said, "Rena, I got this."

She looked over at me, then gave me a terse nod. "Then go get it."

I smiled, turned towards Dina, then announced loud enough for everyone near us to hear, "No one talks to my best friend like that."

After that, I led with my left because everyone was always expecting the right. I felt the cartilage in her nose crunch under the power of my punch, and it was an all-out girl-on-girl cat fight after that, and because Dina wasn't a pussy, she fought back hard. However, too bad for her, she fought like a girl. Years of backyard defense sessions with my dad had taught me how to actually fight, so I swung punches while Dina scratched and pulled hair.

Not sure how long we fought, but it'd been long enough for the police to show up, handcuffs and all.

CHAPTER 24

Nixon ~
It was almost midnight, but I was still wide fucking awake. I was still drowning in regret at what I'd done to Lyric earlier, and the longer that I thought about it, the more I realized that I wouldn't blame her if she'd really meant what she'd said about never wanting to see me again.

Staring at nothing, the fourth tumbler of whiskey went down smoother than the first three, and I wondered if I was drinking to get drunk or just to take the edge off. Tomorrow was a workday, but since I was the boss, I could call in with a hangover, no problem.

I set the empty glass down on the coffee table, then ran my hands up and down my face. Maybe I should just go back to her apartment and beg for forgiveness. Maybe I should just get it over with and tell her that I was pretty sure that I was in love with her. I mean, it had to be love. No man in his right mind would tie himself to a woman that was certifiably crazy if it wasn't love, and more than anything, I wanted to tie myself to Lyrical, no matter her level of insanity.

I also didn't care about her insecurities. Sure, I hoped one day that she'd be able to see herself the way I saw her and know that she was beautiful and loved for exactly the person that she was. Nonetheless, if I had to spend the rest of my life buying her flowers every week and telling her that she was beautiful every night, then I'd do it. I'd do it because nothing and no one had ever made me feel the way Lyrical did.

During my lifetime, I had constructed the most amazing structures in this city, designed the most elegant buildings in this town, and felt the highs of deadlines and the pure elation of standing before a finished masterpiece that had my name on it.

I'd also bedded women with perfect bodies and flawless faces, and I had fucked women that'd had absolutely no limits in bed because they'd thought that my wallet would buy them respectability. I'd been surrounded by models, heiresses, and escorts that had embodied perfection, and had used their feminine talents like weapons.

Still, nothing…not any of my buildings, not any of those women, not the best champagne in the world, not the most expensive meal on the planet…none of it made me feel a fraction of what I felt when I was with Lyrical. Whether it was being buried deep inside her or trying to figure out her crazy, being with her made me feel…*alive*. Like every color would dim and nothing would ever shine if she weren't waiting for me at home at the end of the day.

Fuck, I was in goddamn love.

There was no question about it, and now armed with that certainty, there was only one thing left to do; I had to go beg.

It was almost midnight, so I contemplated just going over to her place dressed as is, in lounge pants and nothing else…well, maybe some shoes, but as I stood up seriously nixing the idea of decent clothing, I heard the sound of my front door unlocking. There were only four people on the planet that had keys to my place, and they were my parents, Jackson, and Lincoln.

I remained where I stood as I watched as Linc pushed open the door, then walked inside. I could feel the beginning tingles of adrenaline start mingling in my blood. If Lincoln was here this late, then something was definitely wrong.

His steps faltered the second that he noticed me standing in the middle of my living room. "Oh, hey, Nix," he greeted. "I just came by to let you know that you owe me twenty-grand."

My brows shot up in surprise. Not what I'd been expecting, but my mind also couldn't conjure up what I could possibly owe Lincoln twenty-grand for. "Oh, really?"

He chuckled, sarcasm in that small act. "Yeah. Really."

I eyed him as he shut the door behind him, then walked into my place until he was standing only a few feet away from me.

I placed my hands on my hips, then said, "Okay, I'll bite. Why do I owe you twenty-thousand dollars, Linc?"

His smirk should have tipped me off, but my mind was so consumed with thoughts of how I was going to beg Lyrical to forgive me that I was a little slow on the uptake. "I just came from the jailhouse where I bailed out your girl and that firecracker friend of hers," he announced as if that little bit of information hadn't just made my entire world shift.

"I'm sorry, what?"

I mean, I had to have heard him wrong, right? He'd meant to say that he bailed Rena out as a favor to Lyrical, which was like a favor to me since Lyric was my girl, right? I mean, there was no fucking way that he said he just bailed Lyrical *and* Rena out of jail.

No. Fucking. Way.

Lincoln flashed me a full-on grin. "Little brother, I fear I must apologize," he said.

Jesus Christ, why did everything have to be a goddamn show with him? "For what?"

"For thinking that you sucked in the sack," he replied, laughing. "If you sucked in bed, then there wouldn't have been a full-blown melee of females fighting over you at Class."

The bottom of my stomach fell out. "What the fuck are you talking about?"

Linc's smile remained plastered on his idiotic face when he started explaining. "I got a call around nine, and it was Lyric using her one phone call to call me." He shrugged a shoulder. "I recognized the number as one of the extensions from the county jail, so I answered, and I bet you can imagine my surprise when it was your girl on the other end."

The fuck?

"What happened? And how in the fuck did she even get your number?"

Linc leaned his ass against the back of the couch, then folded his arms across his chest. "She found my number in the list of attorneys the jail provides for arrests. Her call had gone straight to the answering service, but when they answered, she told them that she was my sister-in-law and that she needed them to patch me through immediately or give her my number outright." I closed my eyes at the thought of how that conversation had gone because she'd obviously gotten Lincoln's direct number. "Anyway, after she proved that she knew enough to appear as if she really was my sister-in-law, they gave her my number when she told them her phone was confiscated, and she didn't have my number memorized."

"Jesus Christ," I hissed, stunned.

This was real.

Lincoln wasn't bullshitting.

"She called me, and I gotta say, Nix, it was the strangest conversation I think I've ever had with somebody in all my life," he chuckled, and I was absolutely positive that it was. "She went on to tell me that it's only assault with the intent to commit bodily harm if a weapon was used and a weapon wasn't used. And then she went on to further explain that if she could just describe to the judge that it was Dina's fault for letting her evil run loose and unchecked, he'd understand. Had Dina never approached her, then she would never have popped her one." Lincoln laughed. "She actually said that, Nixon."

"And Rena?" I had to ask. I wanted to know what all I'd be dealing with.

"That one is a little more tricky," he winced, finally getting serious. "She wasn't involved with the fight, but she was definitely involved with the resisting arrest when she was trying to defend Lyrical."

I ran my hand through my hair. "Goddamn it." I looked at my brother. "Where is she now? Is she at home or at Rena's?"

"I don't know, Nix," he replied. "I walked her to her door, but she could have gone to Rena's after I left. She might feel like they should get their stories straight to avoid the death penalty."

"Not funny, Lincoln," I muttered, glaring at the prick.

"Oh, I disagree," he chortled. "It's very funny."

"So, what are they looking at, Lincoln?"

Now, while I didn't think that their transgressions were going to warrant them the death penalty, assault when I had no idea what kind of criminal record they had-*and let's face it, they probably both had criminal records*-was kind of worrisome.

Lincoln shrugged his shoulder. "I don't think it's that serious, Nix. However, she *is* being charged with assault, public disturbance, and I wouldn't be surprised if they do a psych-hold on her."

"Ha. Ha," I deadpanned.

Lincoln smiled. "The problem is that she hit first, Nixon," he said, getting serious again. "If Dina wants to make a big stink out of this, it could get ugly."

I narrowed my eyes at my brother. "Then you find something on Dina to make sure it doesn't get ugly, Linc," I demanded. "As a matter of fact, find something that makes this go away entirely."

The asshole winked at me. "I'm already on it, little brother."

I ran both my hands through my hair, then back down my face. "Jesus Christ," I mumbled.

"Is she crazy, Nixon?" Linc asked, needing to know what kind of mental mind he might have to defend.

"Nuttier than a fruitcake, Linc," I answered honestly. "Like, if it's hereditary, my children are going to be fucked."

Linc's lip twitched, and I could tell that he was trying not to laugh. "You love her?"

"Every crazy inch of her," I admitted.

Lincoln clapped a hand on my shoulder. "It's going to be okay, Nixon," he assured me. "I'll make my soon-to-be-sister-in-law my priority along with her nutjob friend."

I let out a deep breath, but it didn't help. "Thanks, Linc."

CHAPTER 25

Lyrical ~
I should be sleeping, but I was too amped up to go to bed. I'd spent years trying to keep my big mouth shut and my impulses curbed to avoid the very thing that had just happened.

I had gotten arrested and had ended up in goddamn jail.

Plus, I owed Lincoln St. James twenty-thousand dollars. Like I had twenty-thousand dollars just lying around for occasions like this. While I was sure that he'd take payments, it'd take around eighty-three years to pay that shit off at twenty dollars a month, because that was about all that my budget would allow right now.

Maybe if Rena and I agreed to weekly blowjobs, he'd lower the debt. However, I didn't want to blow Lincoln. I wanted to blow Nixon, and I was pretty sure that Nixon wasn't into sharing, much less sharing with his brother.

The knock on my door wasn't enough to distract me from the impossible math in my head, so I just hollered, "Come in." It could only be Rena, and she needed to do the math with me since her budget was no wealthier than mine.

I mean, what was the price range on blowjobs? Would we have to visit a street corner and get a price listing? Then my mind started giving me a headache with all the logistics popping up all over the place. I mean, there's a blowjob, but then there's deepthroating. Plus, there's swallowing, spitting it out, or letting it fly all over the place. Then, what if the man wanted a deepthroat, but you weren't capable? Did he get a discount? I dropped down on the couch, closed my eyes, then began to rub my temples.

What a disaster.

"So, I'm thinking, I can afford to pay back Lincoln like twenty dollars a month, but it'll take eighty years to pay it all off. And, Rena, hear me out," I implored. "Since half of the bill belongs to you, and you're hot and single, I say we can take turns blowing him to cut down the bill. But you're going to have to actually do him, if he requires it, because…I just don't think I can, Ree."

"What the fuck?"

I yelped, then jumped up off the couch to find a very pissed off Nixon St. James staring at me. "Uh…Nixon, what are you doing here?"

Could this night get any worse?

"Listening to how you plan on blowing my brother for a bail discount, apparently," he growled.

"Well, I don't have twenty-thousand-dollars, Nixon!" I yelled, the night finally getting the better of me. God, didn't the man have any compassion? "What the hell am I supposed to do?!"

He bore down on me. "Not blow my fucking brother!" he thundered. "Who, by the way, doesn't take blowjobs as payment or any other sexual favors!"

"Well, it's not like I *want* to blow him, Nixon," I snapped. "But I don't want to go to prison more."

"Holy Mary, Mother of God," he grumbled, clearly pissed and at his wit's end. "You are not going to prison for a fight unless you are on parole or something like that, Lyric. Are you on parole?"

"Well, no," I admitted.

"Is Rena?"

"No," I mumbled, finally realizing that I may be overreacting a bit. However, in my defense, it'd been a hell of a night.

"I'll handle Linc's bill, Lyric," he stated, still giving me the stink-eye. "You don't have to worry about it."

My eyes widened. Even if we'd been dating seriously, I'd never put that kind of commitment on any man's shoulders. "Nixon, you can't pa-"

"Lyric, so help me God, if you say you'd rather blow my brother than let me pay the bail, I think I will finally succumb to strangling the fuck out of you," he growled.

I took a deep breath, and because he sounded unreasonably serious, I decided to drop the topic of Lincoln's bill. "What are you doing here, Nixon?"

His face relaxed a bit, but I could tell that he was still on edge. "I came to see if you were okay," he answered.

I knew what I was about to say sounded extremely juvenile, but I couldn't help it. I smiled as I said, "Not a scratch on me."

Nixon finally moved past me blowing his brother and chuckled. "Do you want to tell me what happened?"

I dropped back down on the couch, then let out a long breath. "Sure. Take a seat."

Nixon sat down next to me, but before I could recount tonight's festivities, he placed his hand on my knee as he said, "I'm actually here for two reasons, and I'll tell you the second after you've finished telling me what the hell happened tonight, okay?"

I nodded, and then went on to explain how I had ended up at Class, then all the way to how I'd ended up sitting in the county jail. "It was all her fault," I mumbled at the end of my story.

Nixon squeezed my knee, then said, "No, baby. It's actually all my fault."

My shocked gaze latched onto his sincere hazel one. "How do you figure?"

"Everything I told you about Dina being in my apartment is true, Lyric. However, the fault lies in the fact that I never should have let her in my place to begin with. When I think of how I would feel if I showed up at your place and someone you used to mess with was there, with or without his clothes on…fuck, Lyric, Lincoln would be bailing me out of jail, too." Nixon shook his head in remorse and regret. "I never should have let her in my apartment for politeness' sake. Being a gentleman, when I've never really cared if I were one or not before, shouldn't have taken precedence over having another woman in my apartment and how that could look."

My eyes started to water at his apology and need to take responsibility for my insecurities and mental unstableness. "Nixon, you don't ha-"

"No, Lyrical, I do have to," he said, cutting me off. "I have to because I love you. I know it's only been a matter of weeks and way too soon to profess our undying love for one another, but it's the truth. What I feel for you is love. Pure, unconditional, irrevocable love."

Now, stop!

This was the part where you might start to panic because the man that you're pretty sure you're in love with said it first. That panic might set off a chain of events where your uncontrollable emotions might get you committed into the local psychiatric ward where they do serve pudding on Fridays, but that still won't make up for the fact that you're in a mental institution.

So, instead of acting like the completely unbalanced, emotional, neurotic nerd that you were, you throw yourself at the man of your dreams until you're straddling his lap and looking into those perfect hazel eyes of his.

Nixon loved me.

I started playing with the strands of his hair that brushed his neck, and I realized that this was what I wanted. I wanted love with Nixon, but I wanted comfortable, too. I wanted to be comfortable enough to be myself around him and not feel like I was being judged for being a crazy pear.

"I'm crazy, so that's my excuse for falling in love in two weeks. What's your excuse?" I teased.

Nixon laughed, and the sound settled something in my heart. His hands rested on my hips, and they felt like they belonged there. "I don't need an excuse to fall in love with you, Lyric. I just did, and I just am," he stated simply.

"Okay," I whispered. "But I have to ask, Nixon. How much crazy can you take?"

His hands left my hips, then reached up to cradle my face. Nixon leaned up to place a sweet, soft kiss on my lips before saying, "Lyrical, when it comes to you, my crazy threshold is unlimited."

"Are you sure?" I asked. "I mean, don't speak that of which you don't know, Nixon. Things can get pretty crazy around me in case you haven't noticed."

Nixon chuckled. "Oh, I've noticed, baby. Believe me, I've noticed." I smiled as Nixon searched my eyes. "Lyrical, I need you to tell me you believe me about Dina. I swear to you, you're the only woman I want. You're the only woman I'll *ever* want."

I voiced my fears. "How can you be so sure?"

"I'm thirty-three-years-old, Lyric," he said. "I'm not a green boy that's just lost his virginity. I've experienced a lot of things in my life, and nothing and no one I've ever come across has ever made me feel the way you do. I'm in love for the first time in my life, and it's going to be the last, baby."

I let the tears fall because Nixon had seen my crazy, and he still loved me, regardless. So, I didn't need to hide my feelings from him. "I love you, Nixon."

His right hand brushed my face as he smirked. "Enough to risk going to prison since there's no way in hell that I'm letting you blow my brother?" he teased.

The answer was easy.

"Enough to let you pay off your brother, so I don't have to blow him to stay out of prison," I teased back.

Nixon laughed. "Good to know, baby. Good to know."

EPILOGUE

Lyrical – (One Month Later) ~

"Jesus Christ, I can't believe you were going to make me wait for this," Nixon grunted.

"We're at your goddamn parents' house, Nixon," I hissed, doing my best not to scream out loud as his hands tightened on my hips as he rammed into me from behind. We were locked in the guest bathroom while everyone else was outside, enjoying the barbeque put together by the St. James family.

"Believe me, nothing would please my parents more than knowing that their soon-to-be-daughter-in-law was being fucked without protection in their bathroom."

My hands gripped the edge of the counter in a white-knuckle hold. "What are you…oh, God…oh, God…Nixon…right there." I pushed my ass back, helping him reach that spot. "I'm on birth control, you know."

"Oh, fuck, baby," he groaned. "Your pussy's so fucking hot and tight."

"Harder, Nixon," I begged. "Fuck me harder."

Nixon started pounding into me so hard that I knew if anyone entered the house, they'd know what we were doing. Never mind that I'd already met his parents, and they had seemed to like me. It still seemed…uh, inappropriate to let their son fuck me like a cheap whore in their bathroom.

"I'm going to cum, Nixon," I announced as if he didn't already know my body as well as his own.

"Fuck, yeah, Lyric," he grunted. "Cum on my cock, baby. Squeeze my cock and make me cum."

I exploded all over him, and I screamed while I was doing it. If his family came running to see what the panic was, then so be it. Luckily, a few pumps later, Nixon was emptying himself deep inside of me.

"Christ, I never get tired of fucking you," he breathed against the back of my neck.

"Your parents are going to think I'm a hussy that's corrupting their baby boy," I predicted as I tried to regain control of my body and senses.

"My parents already know I'm corrupt, Lyric," he retorted. "You'll be fine."

I laughed. "Get out while I try to make myself presentable."

Nixon pulled out of me, kissed the side of my head, tucked himself back inside his pants, washed his hands, then let me get to putting myself back to rights.

This past month had been a whirlwind of moving too fast, but it'd been wonderful. Nixon had moved me into his apartment the very weekend that we'd made up. Then, as soon as I had moved in, he'd brought me to meet his parents and to officially meet his brothers. Soon, I'd be expected at their monthly family dinners, and it'd been hard not to fall in love with the entire St. James clan immediately.

It'd been the week after that when Lincoln had stopped by to announce that Dina wouldn't be pressing any charges, and that Class didn't want to bother with court appearances when nothing had been broken or damaged.

When I had expressed my shock at Dina not pressing charges, Lincoln had admitted to finding some incriminating information on her that would make her ex-husband clear to close his alimony wallet to her, therefore making her have to actually work for a living. At any rate, I was glad that it was all over.

As for Rena's charges, Lincoln had managed to convince the D.A. that Rena had flipped out because she'd been accidentally touched inappropriately, and that's why she'd been refusing to go with the officer. As soon as he'd made that magical statement, the D.A. had been quick to let it drop since Rena didn't have a criminal history, and Lincoln had promised him it wouldn't happen again.

I finished making myself presentable, then headed back outside. When I stepped off the deck, I saw everyone was already gathered around the table, making their plates.

I made my way over, then sat in the empty spot next to Nixon. The second that I sat down, he handed me the plate that he'd already made for me. I smiled, then couldn't stop myself from leaning my head on his shoulder. It'd only been a couple of months, but this man was just so constantly good to me.

"Thanks, Nixon."

Before Nixon could comment, Felicia St. James asked, "So, Lyric, I don't want to pressure you or anything, but Jackson Sr. and I really need a grandchild to fill our days. So, why don't you guys get to it already?"

"Uh..."

What?

"I understand if you want to be married first, but luckily for you, Jackson may be a retired judge, but he still has the authority to marry couples," she gushed. "Isn't that marvelous?"

"Mom, I thin-"

Mr. St. James stood up, then rubbed his hands together like an evil villain. "I'll go get my things now."

Nixon looked over at me as his father raced towards the house. Ignoring my bewildered expression, he asked, "So, Lyrical...will you marry me?"

What a story to tell our grandchildren, because I said yes.

The End.

ABOUT THE AUTHOR

M.E. Clayton works full-time and writes as a hobby only. She is an avid reader, and with much self-doubt but more positive feedback and encouragement from her friends and family, she took a chance at writing, and the Seven Deadly Sins Series was born. Writing is a hobby she is now very passionate about. When she's not working, writing, or reading, she is spending time with her family or friends. If you care to learn more, you can read about her by visiting the following:

<u>Smashwords Interview</u>

<u>Bookbub Author Page</u>

<u>Goodreads Author Page</u>

OTHER BOOKS

Duets & Series

The Enemy Duet
The Seven Deadly Sins Series
The Enemy Series
Resurrecting the Enemy (Enemy NG Standalone)
The Enemy Next Generation (1) Series
The Enemy Next Generation (2) Series
Embracing the Enemy (Enemy NG Standalone)
The Buchanan Brothers Series
The How to: Modern-Day Woman's Guide Series
The Heavier…Series
The Holy Trinity Series
The Holy Trinity Duet
The Vatican (Holy Trinity NG Standalone)
The Holy Trinity Next Generation (1) Series
The Holy Trinity Next Generation (2) Series
The Eastwood Series
The Blackstone Prep Academy Duet
The Problem Series
The Pieces Series
The Rýkr Duet
The Order of The Cronus Series
The Canvas Duet
When The Series
Expectations Series
The Carmel Springs Series: The Colters
The Carmel Springs Series: The Campions
The Syndicate Duets
The Sports Quintet Series
The Storm Series
The Weight Series
The Through Duet

Standalones

Unintentional
Purgatory, Inc.
My Big, Huge Mistake
An Unexpected Life
Real Shadows
You Again
Merry Christmas to Me
Dealing with the Devil
The Loudest Love

M.E. CLAYTON

Kimmy & The World of Dating
The Right Price
Work Benefits
The Reading
Noctis
Unusual Noises
Murder or Margaritas
Tell Me Your Truths
All of My Life
A Different Kind of Hooker
It's Never *Not* Been You

Made in United States
Orlando, FL
24 September 2024